Mumbai Dreams

DESTINY AND DEATH IN MAXIMUM CITY

Joygopal Podder

V&S PUBLISHER

Published by:

V&S PUBLISHERS

F-2/16, Ansari road, Daryaganj, New Delhi-110002
☎ 23240026, 23240027 • *Fax:* 011-23240028
Email: info@vspublishers.com • *Website:* www.vspublishers.com

Regional Office : Hyderabad
5-1-707/1, Brij Bhawan (Beside Central Bank of India Lane)
Bank Street, Koti, Hyderabad - 500 095
☎ 040-24737290
E-mail: vspublishershyd@gmail.com

Branch Office : Mumbai
Jaywant Industrial Estate, 1st Floor–108, Tardeo Road
Opposite Sobo Central Mall, Mumbai – 400 034
☎ 022-23510736
E-mail: vspublishersmum@gmail.com

Follow us on:

© Copyright: Author
ISBN 978-93-815883-1-4
Edition 2018

Printed at Repro Knowledgecast Limited, Thane

☆☆☆

"Dreams are like stars...you may never touch them, but if you follow them they will lead you to your destiny."

☆☆☆

This book is dedicated to **Priti, Panvi and Piya**. Thanks for inspiring, supporting, encouraging and tolerating.
It has been rightly said – a loving family is the greatest gift God can give...

ALSO BY JOYGOPAL PODDER

CRIME, MYSTERY AND THRILLERS
DECEIVERS
THE INHERITANCE
MILLENNIUM CITY
HIGH ALERT

DRAMA, CRIME AND MYSTERY
SUPERSTAR

TEENAGE DETECTIVE FICTION
THE LANDLORD'S SECRET AND OTHER STORIES

NON FICTION
TRUTH IS STRANGER THAN FICTION

Chapter One

(MARINE DRIVE, MUMBAI)

Police constable Ganesh Chitle loved his early morning beat.

His wife did not share his enthusiasm – for obvious reasons. She had to share with her husband the challenge of waking up at an ungodly hour, six days a week. On her long suffering shoulders fell the essential task of cooking up a substantial breakfast and packing lunch for her hardworking husband – well in time to enable him to attend to his early morning duties on Marine Drive in south Mumbai.

It was the unique location of his beat that sent constable Ganesh Chitle off to work every morning, at 6 am, with a spring in his steps and even the beginnings of a whistle on his lips.

Ganesh loved his job – at least the current assignment. He simply loved walking up and down the promenade of Marine Drive, drinking in the sea view and enjoying the cool early morning breeze wafting in from the ocean.

The morning walkers and joggers posed no problem for the policeman – they gave no trouble. In fact, they added value to the whole atmosphere – which Ganesh Chitle actually found quite electric…

The humble police constable did not, of course, know it then, but the queen's necklace, as the C-shaped sea facing promenade was popularly known, would continue to fascinate him even when he would drive past, several years later, many times every month in his chauffeur driven limousine, security cars ahead and behind him. He would, then, gaze at the ocean with faraway eyes and smile inwardly while remembering his humble beginnings.

But back to the present…

This morning, like every other morning, Ganesh Chitle reached Marine Drive sharp at 6 am He always reached his place of work on time. It was a habit ingrained in him from many years of waking up at the crack of dawn in his modest village home during his childhood – to give him time enough to walk twelve kilometers to school located in the nearest town, so as to reach well before classes began at 7.30 am.

Ganesh now lived in police quarters in Belapur in the Mumbai suburb of Navi Mumbai, the sprawling city extension spread out on either side of the Mumbai-Pune highway. He caught a train every morning to reach the nearest located station to Marine Drive – Victoria Terminus – after a one hour journey in a compartment crowded with commuting Mumbaikers. He would, most mornings, end up standing on his feet the entire trip – all seats occupied and even standing space at a premium.

It was a hectic way to begin the day – but constable Ganesh Chitle had no complaints. The destination was well worth it.

The pavement of the boulevard called Marine Drive curved in a C-shape across its entire three kilometer length, from near the Air India Building and Oberoi Towers Hotel in the south and Chowpatty Beach at the northern end. One side of Marine Drive faced the sparkling waters of the Arabian Sea – and stone benches were neatly laid out at frequent intervals on the pavement on which the citizens of Mumbai as well as tourists could sit and enjoy both the captivating sea view and the enchanting sea breeze.

Ganesh Chitle was, this morning, a contented man. His stomach was happily full from the hearty breakfast of kanda pohay, a Maharashtrian snack made from flattened rice and onion shreds, and hot pao bhaji – a bun like bread with a vegetable preparation, which his wife had prepared for him that morning. His other needs had been met by his wife only the night before, in a sensuous coupling of bodies that still sent him to heaven even after twelve years of marriage.

His two small children were bright and healthy – and doing well in school. What more could a man want?

At which point his pleasant reflections were disturbed by the sight of two horizontal figures wrapped up in sheets and lying on two of the stone benches – one bench each. They appeared to be asleep and looked extremely comfortable.

Ganesh Chitle tapped his police stick on the ground. He did not like this. The stone benches on the Marine Drive promenade were meant for sitting on – not sleeping on. The morning walkers and joggers would have every right to complain to *him*, the nearest policeman – and Ganesh knew from past experience that such complaints, particularly from the elderly, could be quite vocal, shrill and distasteful.

He raised his stick and poked one of the sleeping figures, initially lightly and then slightly more aggressively, until the young man surfaced from his slumber.

"Get up! You can't sleep on this bench!" Ganesh was curt but not rudely so. He knew what it felt to be homeless…

The young man got to his feet, looking slightly dazed with broken sleep.

"Wake up your friend and take off from here!" ordered Ganesh. "Let me not catch you sleeping here again!"

The young man recovered his senses quickly – and crossed over to the other bench and shook the other young man. "Wake up, Dev! The cops are here…"

Dev immediately woke up. A thin face with a bright smile, the hair on the head completely disheveled, greeted constable Ganesh Chitle. "Good morning, inspector!" greeted the young man called Dev. "Thanks for waking us up! We were oversleeping – we'll be late for our meetings!'

"Don't be over smart!" responded Ganesh with irritation. "And its 'constable' not 'inspector'!"

"No matter – you'll soon be inspector," said Dev, with remarkable foresight. He scrambled to his feet and began stuffing the sheet he had wrapped around himself, to take protection from the cold night sea breeze, into his cloth bag that was lying next to the bench. His companion did likewise.

"Where are you boys from?" asked Ganesh Chitle. He could make out that two were very young, probably in their early twenties, not more.

"Dehradun," replied Dev, combing his hair swiftly.

"You guys are very far from home, aren't you? You've come to Mumbai to become film stars?" asked Ganesh knowingly.

Dev pointed at the other young man with his comb. "Sanjeev is the one who aims to make it big in films! I have other ambitions…"

Constable Ganesh Chitle's eyes twinkled. He quite liked this young man called Dev. "What ambition can be bigger than becoming a film star?"

Dev became quiet. He looked around him. Then he turned and stared northwards – towards Malabar Hills and beyond, his eyes seeming to soar over the towering skyscrapers of Mumbai and reach out to far off places like Juhu and Bandra…

"One day," said Dev softly – so softly that Ganesh Chitle wondered if had heard right, "this city will be mine…"

Chapter Two

(SELF DESTRUCTION)

It would take a dozen lifetimes for anyone to amass two million followers on twitter – and yet superstar actor, sex god, the highest paid entertainer in Indian history, playboy, alcoholic and drug abuser Abhay Kaushik had managed to achieve this feat in less than six months.

It was six months ago that the meltdown had begun – after Abhay's much touted big budget science fiction film 'Merchants of Death' had bombed at the box office.

Nobody could point a finger at the exact cause for the failure of the film – and that was because there were so many of them. Critics and trade pundits alike had predicted doom well before the film's release. But Abhay was unmindful. He had personally chosen the script, the star cast, the producer and the director. He, the golden goose of the Indian film industry, knew exactly what worked and what did not work. And he had put together a film that would *definitely* work – his genius in knowing what the Indian and NRI audiences wanted, had surely ensured that.

After all, he, Abhay Kaushik, had not become a superstar just by chance and luck – it was his genius and knowledge of public taste that had propelled him to the dizzying heights of stardom and kept him at the top for over a decade. Or so he felt.

He had been wrong on all counts. 'Merchants of Death' had found it difficult to draw in the crowds. The first day following the release of the film had witnessed packed theatres – Abhay's power to ensure a magnificent 'initial' had ensured this, even though the pre-release reports had all panned the movie.

But, after the first day, word of mouth publicity (rather 'negative' publicity) and terrible reviews killed the film. Nobody went to see it –

theatres were empty of audiences (except those few who went for a 'laugh' or to see how far the God of Bollywood had fallen). Abhay had never been able to take stardom in his stride. Great fame and wealth had enlarged his ego to bizarre proportions. His public rantings had fed an entire industry of pulp journalists for years. Now, after the great debacle of his latest film – on which he had staked so much prestige – Abhay Kaushik simply lost it.

The funny thing was – the more erratic Abhay became, the greater was his fame and notoriety, and the more valuable a property he was seen to have become in the eyes of those who financed and made money from the Indian entertainment industry.

During the past six months, Abhay Kaushik has become a hot-blooded Bollywood bad boy. His television interviews were the stuff of legends. "I'm tired of pretending that I'm not special. I'm tired of pretending that I'm not a total bitching rock star from Mars!" declared Abhay Kaushik in one now very famous interview over national television a little over three months ago. In another recent interview aired on the nation's leading entertainment television channel, Abhay declared: "I'm on a drug. It's called Abhay Kaushik. It's not available to anybody else because if you try it, you will die!"

Abhay's newspaper and magazine interviews carried titles like: "I always win" and "I have tiger blood running through my veins".

Abhay's over-the-top partying and many alcohol and drug binges were regular page three items in leading newspapers – often overshadowing major political dramas.

Then, two months ago, the Council of Film Producers had announced that the previously declared 'Lifetime Achievement' award announced earlier in the year in favor of Abhay Kaushik had been withdrawn on grounds of his "deteriorating condition and escalating erratic conduct."

Since then, Abhay Kaushik had become one of the biggest names in the planet – his bizarre conduct faithfully followed by millions of Indians, NRIs and even non-Indians on twitter, facebook, Google, online news portals, television channels and newspapers and magazines.

What was most fascinating about the whole public drama was that, unwittingly, by his very bizarre conduct and increasing madness,

Abhay Kaushik had given the world a master class in modern media promotion.

It pays to be bad – and mad. For all his troubles, Abhay Kaushik was selling more than he had ever done before…

Chapter Three

Dev Sharma and Sanjeev Raina, close friends from Dehradun who had arrived in Mumbai by train only the previous day and had nowhere to stay and not enough money to afford accommodation in a guest house, headed for the world famous Taj Mahal Hotel to freshen up. The Taj was about a twenty minute or so walk from Marine Drive and faced the historical Gateway of India, through which British monarchs and their heirs used to first enter the country after disembarking from the ships which had brought them half way round the world for this visit to the great jewel of Britain's colonial empire.

Dev Sharma prided himself on his ability to research. Dehradun had good internet connectivity – and Dev had used every opportunity to master the art of exploiting the facilities offered by online search engines.

Google searches had revealed to him that the Taj Mahal Hotel had huge bathrooms behind the lobby – which were used by many members of the general public possessing gumption and adequate awareness, to relieve and freshen themselves whenever they happened to be in the vicinity in the course of their daily routines. This is where Dev led an apprehensive Sanjeev immediately after their eviction from the Marine Drive benches by constable Ganesh Chitle.

The duo eventually emerged from the Taj Mahal Hotel bathed, brushed and ready for action. The tall and imposing thickly mustached guards at the main entrance actually saluted them on their way out…

Dev and Sanjeev parted on the road outside the Taj Mahal Hotel. Sanjeev was headed for the Deep Mala Studios complex in Chembur, a half-an-hour bus ride away, where he had an audition to attend. Dev was headed just across the road to the jetty next to the Gateway of

India, from where he would board a ferry which would take him across the Arabian Sea to Ali Baugh, located forty minutes or so away.

The friends promised to meet in Marine Drive in the evening.

Dev chose the sea route since it was more convenient. Ali Baugh is only about twenty kilometers away from south Mumbai by the sea route. By road it is a three hour drive from Mumbai as the route winds north from the Mumbai peninsula to the suburb of Navi Mumbai and then, half way to Pune, curves and moves south along the mainland coast.

The ageing catamaran was half full – yet Dev chose to climb the rickety ladder to the upper deck so that he could enjoy the open sea unhindered by an enclosed space and also by co-passengers blocking the view. For a young man coming from a landlocked town like Dehradun, this sea ride, though short, was heaven.

Dev also liked to squeeze out the maximum pleasure from every experience in life…

At the Ali Baugh jetty, Dev boarded a bus for the town (the price was included in the ferry ticket).

Although it was his first ever visit to Ali Baugh, Dev Sharma knew exactly where he was headed. He had come all the way to Mumbai from Dehradun with Sanjeev with a specific game plan in mind and after doing a lot of research through the internet and in libraries. After disembarking at the bus stand in Ali Baugh town, Dev did not dawdle, but approached the auto-rickshaw stand. "I want to go to the fort," he informed the first driver he saw.

"That's just walking distance from here, my friend." The auto-rickshaw driver was honest – he had no intention of fleecing a simple young man.

"Not Kolaba Fort," replied Dev, referring to the three hundred and fifty year old military fortification located just a kilometer into the sea from the main town. "Take me to the Kasturi Fort."

The auto-rickshaw driver eyed Dev warily. "Are you sure? Its twenty kilometers from here. There's no habitation nearby. And you'll need me to bring you back – you'll have no other option. It'll be expensive."

"I'm sure." They haggled – and arrived at an amicable figure, which was still far beyond Dev's means. Dev shrugged to himself – he would need to invest a bit to make money. There was no such thing as a free lunch in this world...

It was late afternoon by the time Dev Sharma returned to Ali Baugh town. He paid off the auto-rickshaw driver and boarded the bus to the same jetty where he had landed from Mumbai – the Mandwa jetty. Dev just about managed to catch the last ferry back to Mumbai at 6 pm

The cell phone connectivity was lost while the ferry was out at sea – but was restored as the catamaran neared the jetty next to the Gateway of India. Dev's phone rang. It was an excited sounding Sanjeev. "We have a place to stay! We won't have to camp on the Marine Drive benches tonight!"

Dev was confused. "Can we afford it?"

"It's free!" As Dev disembarked from the ferry, Sanjeev told him the address he would have to go to.

Dev's eyes widened. "That's nearby – right here in Colaba! How did you manage a free apartment here? This place is posh!"

"It was simple, really," replied Sanjeev with a laugh. "I just happened to be in the right place at the right time! Let's meet at the apartment quickly – and I'll tell you. There's a caretaker there who's been told we're coming!"

"But still, how *did* you manage?"

"If you must know – I discovered a fire..."

Chapter Four

(GETTING DRUNK)

Abhay Kaushik, the top film star of Bollywood, was in full form. He had arrived very late at Deep Mala Studios – and had then proceeded to do everything but work.

Abhay was scheduled to have a song picturised on him that day. It was an energetic dance number involving many dancers and junior artistes. The only problem was that Abhay Kaushik did not feel very energetic that morning – even though he had woken up very late and had taken his own sweet time to reach the studios, keeping over thirty people waiting with his severe late coming.

Abhay reached Deep Mala studios at lunch time – and promptly took refuge in his enormous vanity van. "Tell the production assistants I'm very hungry," he instructed his secretary Ravinder Guha.

A lavish luncheon spread was promptly organised. Abhay was not really very hungry – the talk of hunger pangs had only been a ploy to delay going on the sets. He picked at his food listlessly and made a face when informed that the underproduction film's young director had come over to the vanity van to meet him.

The director was young – it was his first film – but he was no pushover. Vijay Bhardawaj was talented and dynamic – and did not suffer fools gladly. He had taken on Abhay Kaushik because his producer had insisted. As a first time director, Vijay could hardly have refused his producer's wishes. The producer had wanted a bankable and newsworthy star, no matter how erratic that star had become in recent times, to balance out the new director who would not have a name or fame to draw in the crowds, and Vijay possessed enough business savvy to understand this. But he still needed to ensure a degree of discipline on the sets.

Today's delay was causing a huge financial loss to the producer. It could not be tolerated. Vijay would have to beard the lion – he would need to do some hard talking with the superstar.

His was not a very enviable position. Vijay wished he was elsewhere.

"I do hope you are not feeling unwell," he said to Abhay Kaushik, not feeling as solicitous as he tried to sound.

"I don't know," replied Abhay, not looking at the director but concentrating on a number flashing on his cell phone.

"The set is ready for your shot. If you're up to it, we'd all appreciate it if you could join us for the shoot."

Something in the young director's tone made Abhay look up suddenly. "Are you telling me what to do?"

This was it. Vijay Bhardawaj put his career at stake and replied: "Yes."

Abhay Kaushik was at least ten years older than the young director. He was tall and muscular, as befitting a hero of the Hindi film industry. But he suddenly felt very small in front of the debutant film director. He did not like this.

"Who do you think you are – pulling your weight like this?" said Abhay Kaushik, raising his voice. "Have you forgotten who I am?"

"No, I haven't forgotten! That's why I have been so patient so far!"

Abhay's face turned almost purple. Ravinder Guha, who was present and standing on the sidelines of this confrontation, backed away slightly, as if a volcano was about to erupt.

"You nut case!" shouted Abhay Kaushik. "If you think that I'm going to hang around taking shit from a wannabe like you, then take a chill pill and get lost! I'll do what I want, when I want, how I want!"

Vijay got to his feet. "In that case, you're no longer working on my film Mr. Abhay Kaushik!" He stormed out of the film star's vanity van.

Abhay stared after the young director – his eyes blazing. Then he looked at his secretary and pointed at the fridge. "Get out all the bottles of beer stored in that fridge!" he ordered.

Ravinder Guha quickly complied. He also placed a bottle opener on the table, next to the seven beer bottles, as well as a couple of packets of expensive cigarettes and a lighter.

"Go away!" ordered Abhay Kaushik. "I wanna be alone!"

As Ravinder Guha made a hurried exit from the vanity van, Abhay Kaushik grabbed a beer bottle and poured the contents down his throat. "Let's see how they can make me do that dance scene now…" he murmured to himself, while lighting a cigarette.

Chapter Five

(FIRE)

Sanjeev Raina was getting sick of waiting.

He had reached Deep Mala Studios on the dot at 10 am – the time when auditions were scheduled to start. So had about a hundred other young men.

Sanjeev got his first big lesson in life – he was not as important as he had thought he was.

When Sanjeev had received the invitation to attend the auditions in Mumbai, for a minor role in debutant director Vijay Bhardawaj's upcoming film, in response to his application sent in reply to an advertisement in a film magazine, he had been ecstatic. In a short time, practically everybody in Dehradun got to know that Sanjeev was going to Mumbai to join films – that he had been *called* to Mumbai to join films. Today was the day Sanjeev Raina of Dehradun fell back to the earth with a thud. Today he realised that he was just one of more than a hundred wannabe actors from Mumbai and all over the country, some with film and theatre experience and some, like him, with no formal acting background, who had applied against the advertisement and had been shortlisted for a preliminary audition.

Sanjeev now realised that his chance of getting the much coveted role was one in a hundred – if even that.

The wait had been endless, the form filling exercise tedious, the endless self-rehearsing of the lines given to him tiring and, after some time, boring – the tension unbearable. It was late in the afternoon – and only about thirty young men had been auditioned by the assistants to the debutant director.

Vijay Bhardawaj, himself, was slated to meet a very limited number of finalists sometimes in the future – not today.

Sanjeev Raina's serial number was sixty-five. His turn was clearly several hours away. Tired of sitting around and doing nothing, Sanjeev finally decided to go exploring.

He had never visited the inside of a film studio before. Today seemed a good day to go sightseeing inside one of the biggest film studios in the country. His learnings would come in useful in his fledgling career – or so he hoped.

Sanjeev slipped away from the hall in which the actor hopefuls had been waiting since morning and quietly and unobtrusively began visiting the different sets erected inside the studio complex.

Film scenes were being shot on some of the sets. The bustle and high energy activity was fascinating to watch. Sanjeev, of course, could not get close enough to watch the actual acting out of scenes by the leading and supporting actors in the different films that were on the floors of Deep Mala Studios that day – but even his distant glimpses and short stay on the periphery of the different film sets, amongst the crowd of onlookers and crew, was instructive enough.

The day's visit to Deep Mala Studios was beginning to finally pay off – even if the original purpose was still to be achieved…

There was an another studio in the complex in which not much was happening, even though a huge and glitzy set had been erected and many dozens of people – many dressed up in similar looking glamorous clothes – were sitting about listlessly. There was an air of resignation all around – as if patience had worn out and all knew very clearly now that not much activity would be happening that day.

There was a large crew hanging about. Cameras were in place. Lighting had evidently been positioned earlier in the day in readiness for cameras to roll. There was even a tall crane on which was fixed a camera about sixty feet from the ground – in readiness to capture some aerial view shots.

But no action was happening on the floor.

Sanjeev's puzzlement was soon solved when he saw a bearded young man with pony tail neatly tied behind his head and wearing jeans and an open necked white shirt, storm into the hall and stride up to the area where a few senior looking crew members were sitting. Sanjeev recognised one of the crew members as the famous dance director Wasim Razak.

Sanjeev also recognised the pony tailed young man – it was none other than the director Vijay Bhardawaj himself.

"Abhay has decided to play difficult today!" Sanjeev heard Vijay Bhardawaj exclaim to the group of senior crew members. "He's not going to shoot his scenes!"

Several people began speaking all at once – and Sanjeev made a quick exit from that particular studio...

Outside, the afternoon sun was high up in the sky and the air was hot and humid.

Sanjeev forgot about the commotion in the studio inside as he surveyed the huge vanity vans parked in the open air compound he had just stepped into.

Sanjeev knew all about film star vanity vans. This was what he aspired for, a huge high top vanity van with luxurious interiors all for himself – the symbol of success that would, one day, surely be his.

There were six vanity vans parked in the compound. Four were Swaraz Mazda's. Sanjeev's attention was drawn to the two biggest, which were Volvo – and had clearly had a lot of work done on them by designers.

Oh, how he wanted to see one from inside!

Sanjeev knew, from the extensive reading that he had done of film magazines and while surfing on the internet, that the vanity vans assigned to or belonging to top film stars were, literally, mini palaces on wheels, with luxurious drawing rooms, bed rooms, high-tech toilets, dressing rooms and – in a couple of famous cases – even gyms. He longed to see one from inside...

Could he see one from inside?

Sanjeev snuffed out the thought as soon as it struck him – but the thought returned like a shamefaced dog that had gone missing from its master's house and scratched at the door of his mind again, asking for a second opportunity.

Sanjeev considered. There was some activity going on around the four Swaraj Mazda vanity vans. People were going in and out carrying things like dresses and food. A television crew had actually set up equipment outside one – a star interview would soon be commencing, it appeared.

But the two giant Volvo vanity vans were enveloped in silence. Were they empty?

There was only one way to find out. Squaring his shoulders, Sanjeev determinedly and with a confident air about him, strode up to the nearest Volvo vanity van and quickly grabbed the door handle – hoping that nobody was staring at him.

The door swung open!

Sanjeev could not believe his luck – he quickly stepped into the van.

Inside, he found himself in a very large, wood paneled sitting area, furnished very comfortably with plush sofas and designer side tables. There was a large flat screen television fixed to one wall. This vanity van was certainly posh! Hearing no sounds from the interiors of the van, Sanjeev decided to venture further in his exploration.

He crossed a small corridor – and was about to enter into what looked like a big dressing and make-up room, when he smelt smoke.

Then he *saw* the smoke – it was billowing out, in small strands, from under the door he was passing!

Sanjeev also thought he heard a faint moan. It was coming from behind the door!

Sanjeev did not waste time in further thought. He grabbed the door handle. The door was not locked. He swung open the door and stepped into what looked like a bedroom. There was a huge bed in the room. The bed was on fire. And on the bed was lying a man…

Sanjeev took all this in – and then acted. Coughing from the smoke, he jumped on the bed, grabbed the man lying on it, and half dragged and half carried him out of the room.

By now, the smoke – and a bit of the fire – had spread to the sitting area. The van would soon be a blazing inferno!

The man was limp – and draped all over Sanjeev. He was a muscular fellow – and it took all of Sanjeev's energies to simply hold and drag and carry the limp form to the main door of the van. He reached the door and kicked it open.

As smoke billowed out from the open door of the Volvo vanity van, people exclaimed and rushed towards it from all directions. The television crew had just begun filming the interview of a rising young actress in front of her vanity van. The cameraman turned instinctively, along with his camera, toward the direction of the huge commotion – and promptly caught on film the scene of a disheveled Sanjeev Raina emerging from the burning Volvo vanity van supporting and dragging out with him from the blazing vehicle the limp and barely conscious form of the superstar Abhay Kaushik…

Chapter Six

(RIVALRY)

The man was in his early fifties. He lay placidly on the hospital bed in the VIP suite located in the exclusive wing of the prestigious Aashirwad Hospital in central Mumbai.

Two bulky and uniformed security men stood guard outside the door of the suite, screening all those who sought to enter the room, including doctors and nurses. One of the wealthiest men of India lay on the hospital bed inside the room – kidnapping for ransom was always a real danger to be considered and protected against.

The middle aged man lying on the bed was Deepak Patel, Chairman of Progressive Constructions Limited. Towering over him, next to the bed, was a state-of-the-art haemodialysis machine. Two tubes ran from the machine and into the cimino fistula in the upper left arm of Deepak Patel. The fistula had been created by a short surgical procedure that had joined an artery and vein in Deepak Patel's upper arm to permit easier withdrawal of blood from his body for the thrice-a-week haemodialysis procedure which he had to religiously undergo in order to stay alive.

Deepak Patel's kidneys were dead. They had ceased to function three years ago after a severe bout of hypertension – which had been brought on by a takeover attempt of his company by Rajiv Rastogi, owner of a rival real estate company called Buildtech Limited – and reputed to be a front man for the dreaded Don of Dubai. Deepak Patel's kidneys had always been under pressure as a result of his diabetic condition – the attack of hypertension had finished them off.

In medical terms, he had suffered, three years ago, acute renal failure.

Ever since then, for the last three years, a haemodialysis machine had done the work of his kidneys. Three times a week, in a four-hour-long procedure each time, the unclean blood was flushed out from his body, the impurities in the blood were removed – and then the blood was recycled back into his body. In a simultaneous procedure, in addition to removing the waste products like creatinine and urea from his blood, accumulated water was also removed from his body in a process called ultra filtration (UF).

He always lost weight during dialysis – which was a good thing, he sometimes joked.

The regular dialysis procedure was actually quite a strain on the body – and it had adversely affected Deepak Patel's heart condition, making a kidney transplant operation an inadvisable procedure.

Today, Deepak Patel's twenty-three-year old daughter Sunita Patel, Managing Director and Chief Executive of Progressive Constructions Limited, sat by his side, on a chair next to the bed. She held a BlackBerry phone in her hand – which she had just disconnected. "Rajiv Rastogi is bidding for the same tie-up!" she announced.

Deepak Patel looked calmly at his daughter. "He never gives up, does he?"

"He won't give up, papa," responded Sunita, "until he has beaten us in the market place and has brought us to our knees so that he can take over Progressive Constructions!"

"Beating Progressive Constructions is not going to be an easy task..."

"But he's constantly trying to outsmart us one way or the other!" complained Sunita. "Now he's trying to take away the Daffodils Resorts tie-up from us – right from under our noses!"

"How?"

"He's offering what he says are better sites for the resort project. He's trying to seduce the Daffodils people by claiming ownership of better properties on which they can establish a resort that will be more tourist friendly." She raised the BlackBerry phone in her hand. "The call I just got was from one of our managers – who got information from a Buildtech manager that the visiting delegation from Daffodils Resorts had been taken to Madh Island today to inspect a property that Ravi Rastogi claims can beat any site that we may have to offer!"

Deepak Patel looked surprised – and slightly pained. "The Daffodils people never told us about these feelers from Buildtech?"

"No, papa."

"This does not look good…" Deepak Patel contemplated the two tubes, filled with his blood, which were connected to his upper arm at one end and to the haemodialysis machine at the other end. His thrice a week haemodialysis procedure not only sapped him of energy but gave him very little time to *personally* attend to challenges posed by rivals – like the present one. Poor Sunita had a heavy burden to carry…

"Our sites on the coast north and south of Mumbai are not bad," continued Sunita, "but neither are they exceptional. We need a *clincher* of a site – but I have no clue where to find one."

Deepak Patel sighed and resigned himself to face another possible disappointment. "The Daffodils tie-up can earn us a lot of prestige – and also open up the hospitality sector to us. We *need* this collaboration in order to implement our diversification plans. Let's hope that the Daffodils delegation does not get seduced away from us!"

"I'm praying, papa – I'm praying…"

Chapter Seven

(SAVIOUR)

Sanjeev Raina from Dehradun was a hero. His face was all over the television news channels – which kept on playing the dramatic footage of Sanjeev staggering out of a burning vanity van, holding on to a practically unconscious Abhay Kaushik, the heartthrob and bad boy of the Indian film industry.

Sanjeev had displayed exceptional bravery and saved a life – not just *any* life but that of a superstar.

The only reason that Dev had missed all this excitement in the electronic media was because he had been busy in the interiors of the island of Ali Baugh, far away from television screens, and then was travelling across the sea by ferry to get back to Mumbai.

Sanjeev had become the toast of Mumbai while Dev had been visiting Ali Baugh. He became a celebrity the moment he stepped out of the burning vanity van.

As emergency teams went into crisis management mode to contain and diffuse the fire in Abhay Kaushik's vanity van, medical help was immediately provided to the superstar himself. Abhay had drunk himself silly with seven bottles of beer and had inadvertently set fire to his bed with a carelessly dropped cigarette while he was in his drunken stupor. That chain of events was soon established – there were enough empty bottles of beer and packets of cigarettes in the half burnt bedroom of the vanity van to help piece together the events that led to the fire…

Abhay himself was none the worse for his experience – thanks to the timely rescue by Sanjeev – but he was still in a drunken stupor even after his rescue, though with enough understanding still left to know that somebody had saved his life. Abhay was quickly dispatched to the nearest hospital for rest and recovery under strict medical supervision.

As a slightly overwhelmed Sanjeev was interviewed by excited journalists and congratulated by the cast and crew of the several films that were being shot in Deep Mala Studios that day, two men stood on the sidelines and carefully observed the unfolding euphoria. One of them was Vijay Bhardawaj and the other was his producer Sudershan Joshi.

The news of the exchange of hot words between his film's director and lead actor had quickly reached Sudershan Joshi in his suite of offices inside the Deep Mala studios complex. Sudershan had immediately dropped all other work and rushed down to the studio floor to meet Vijay and seek to resolve this developing crisis that could easily derail his film and his business.

The two men were discussing the erratic behaviour of their lead actor and arguing over whether to continue with Abhay in the lead role or otherwise (Vijay was adamant that the superstar was to be sacked but Sudershan was not so sure) when news of the fire in the vanity van reached them. Now, after having ensured the dousing of the flames and the provision of medical attention to Abhay, they were witnessing the aftermath…

"This boy Sanjeev did a really brave thing today!" observed Sudershan. "Who is he? Is he working in some film here?"

"I've been told that he had come for today's auditions…" replied Vijay, stroking his beard.

"Was he good in the auditions?"

"His chance is yet to come."

Sudershan Joshi looked thoughtful. "This young man has suddenly become very popular because of his brave act. It'll all die down, of course, in a couple of days – unless somebody keeps it alive…"

Vijay stared hard at his producer and said: "Are you thinking what I am thinking? Can we encash on this young man's new found fame for our film?"

"Why not?" asked Sudershan Joshi simply.

Vijay stroked his beard again. "Yes, why not?"

Chapter Eight

(A PLACE TO STAY)

Sanjeev was concluding his story: "All of a sudden, these two men approached me while I was giving another two minute interview to one more television channel. One of the men was the director Vijay Bhardawaj, for whose film I had gone to audition. The other man introduced himself as Sudershan Joshi, the film's producer." Sanjeev looked at Dev and grinned from ear to ear. "They offered me a major role in the film!"

Dev was delighted. "What a wonderful break! You deserve it, Sanjeev! I'm very happy for you!"

Sanjeev rolled his eyes upwards. "It's all fate and destiny!"

Dev was highly amused. "I had thought that we had taken our destiny into our *own hands* when we decided to leave Dehradun and come to an unknown territory like Mumbai to seek out our fortunes! Since when have you begun believing in fate?"

"Since this afternoon!" replied Sanjeev firmly. "I was put in the right place at the right time so that I could do the right thing which would get me the right break!"

Dev stretched himself out on the leather sofa in the drawing room of the Colaba apartment and replied seriously. "No, my friend – that's where you're wrong! It was your passion for becoming a film star and desire to check out film star lifestyle that made you steal into Abhay Kaushik's vanity van. It was your courage and humanity that made you risk your life to rescue Abhay. You could easily have run out of the van and left Abhay to his fate!"

Sanjeev shrugged his shoulders. "I don't agree – but let's not spoil the fun of this evening in this grand apartment by arguing. There'll be enough time for that later…"

"Sure! And this apartment? This came with the role?"

"Yes! When I told Sudershan and Vijay that I had no place to stay except the Marine Drive benches, they were shocked. They said that an actor playing a major role in their film could not sleep on the streets – the movie would attract publicity of the wrong kind. So they asked me to take over this apartment temporarily – it is owned by Sudershan's production company – and they told me that they would make book adjustments to show that our stay here would be part of my overall remuneration for acting in the film…"

Dev was impressed. "You've certainly hit big time! They know about me?"

"Yes. They've no issues with you staying here. They just don't want us getting girls into this place and having wild parties, that's all."

Dev nearly choked over the glass of orange juice that he had been drinking. Girls! Wild parties! *As if…*

Dev and Sanjeev had come to Mumbai to build big futures. They had left home and hearth in comfortable Dehradun – that lovely little town at the foothills of the Himalayas where they had been born and raised and had spent all their lives, so far – so that they could exploit the big city opportunities that Mumbai had to offer to the ambitious. There would be no time for girls and wild parties!

In thinking this, Dev Sharma once again threw a challenge at fate…

31

Chapter Nine

(THE MESSAGE)

The next morning, Dev got to work.

Sanjeev had a free day – he had been called to Deep Mala Studios for a meeting with Sudershan Joshi and Vijay Bhardawaj only the next day. So he had a whole day to kill. All his attempts to tempt Dev to accompany him to Juhu Beach for a day of leisure and pleasure, however, were in vain.

"You've embarked on your journey on all four gears, my friend! But I'm yet to get into first gear!" Dev reminded Sanjeev. "Besides, I spent practically the whole of yesterday by the sea – in Ali Baugh. I can do with a break from the coastline, thank you!"

So Sanjeev resigned himself to a day sprawled in front of the TV – with coke and chips for company. He was in no mood to explore the sprawling city of Mumbai alone, without Dev by his side. There would be time enough in the near future to see the city sights through the windows of his chauffeur driven limousine, thought Sanjeev to himself.

He switched on the DVD player and began watching a blockbuster Abhay Kaushik movie.

Dev hit the computer in the study of the Colaba apartment. He had his game plan ready. He rolled up his sleeves and got to work.

The computer had internet connectivity. This saved Dev the bother of going to an internet café to work. He quickly searched out the website of Progressive Constructions Limited. He did not bother with the 'home' page of the website – but clicked through to the 'contact us' site.

Dev quickly scanned the names of the senior managers and departmental heads listed in the 'management structure' page of the 'contact us' site. He did not find what he wanted. He clicked on to the 'board members' page. Sure enough, she was listed: Sunita Patel,

Managing Director and Chief Executive of Progressive Constructions Limited. But no email address was mentioned against her name. In fact, no email address was mentioned against the name of any board member. This, Dev knew, was a normal practice in any company website – members of the board of directors were protected from unsolicited emails seeking favours and patronage by simply not having their email addresses listed.

Still, Dev had been hoping...

He now needed to puzzle out the email address of Sunita Patel. Dev went back to the 'management structure' page...

Yes, there was a pattern. There was *always* a pattern. IT managers of big companies had pretty unimaginative minds when it came down to creating a company email identity on the captive server. The head of construction was a gentleman called Randhir Sobti. His email id was randhir.sobti@progressiveconstructions.org.

Dev browsed further. Yes, sure enough, the head of human relations was called Govind Wankhade. His email id? It was, what else, govind.wankhade@progressiveconstructions.org.

Dev had his answer – he decided to take the risk. He typed his password and opened his email account.

"Dear Ms. Sunita Patel," Dev typed, "I'm sorry for this intrusion but this is not spam mail. This is not a prank either. I know from the newspaper reports and from news items on the internet that you are looking for a tie-up with the world renowned Daffodils Resorts from the US. Your company will provide the property on which their first Indian resort will be built. The resort will be a joint venture. I know you need a good site to please the Daffodils officials. I can also guess that you will have competitors who will also be vying to grab this tie-up away from you. I can show you an unbeatable site – if you trust me, that is!"

Dev signed off with his full name. In the 'subject' box he typed: AN UNBEATABLE SITE FOR YOUR TIE-UP WITH DAFFODILS RESORTS. In the 'to' box he typed out, without a second thought: sunita.patel@progressiveconstructions.org.

He positioned the cursor on the 'send' button and pressed – all the while muttering a prayer under his breath.

As the mail to Sunita Patel left his 'outbox' Dev waited with bated breath. A minute passed, then another. The mail to Sunita Patel had not bounced back! He had guessed the email address correctly – or so he hoped. There was still a chance that, although the email address was correct, the message would be first seen by a secretary with access to this official email account of Sunita Patel – and that *this* functionary would decide whether to delete Dev's message, regarding it as a prank, or pass it on to the boss.

However, Dev also knew that a person like Sunita Patel would ordinarily use an internet friendly BlackBerry or a similar telephone instrument on which she could access her email while on the move. In which case, she would see the mail. How she would react was the million dollar question...

Dev decided not to fret. He already had a list of several other 'prospects' among the real estate tycoons of Mumbai to whom he would approach in case Sunita Patel did not bite the bait. But he hoped it would be Sunita – the proposal he had sent her met her needs perfectly.

Dev switched off the computer, joined Sanjeev in front of the television and got engrossed in the on screen heroics of Abhay Kaushik.

Chapter Ten

(TALKING BUSINESS)

Sunita Patel read the email on her BlackBerry. She immediately telephoned the head of constructions of Progressive Constructions Limited, Randhir Sobti – and also forwarded Dev's mail to his email address.

When Dev went back to the computer and checked his email after one hour, a reply was waiting for him. It was from Randhir Sobti. "Can we talk?"

Randhir Sobti had helpfully typed out his mobile number in the mail. Dev called him.

"Is this some kind of a prank?" Randhir Sobti's opening remarks were not friendly.

"No. And if that's the kind of attitude you have, then let's not waste time talking any further!"

"Wait, wait!" Randhir Sobti's instructions were clear – to fully investigate the offer and report back. He could not afford to turn off the caller by being rude. "O.K. I'll cut out the disbelief – tell me what you have on offer…"

"There's nothing to tell – only to show. You and your boss will have to accompany me to the site," responded Dev firmly.

There was a pause as Randhir Sobti thought this over. "All right," he said finally, "I'll go with you to the site and see what' on offer."

"I don't think you heard me clearly. *Both* you and your boss will accompany me to the site – or else there will be no visit!"

Dev held his breath. He had just made a big gamble – perhaps wagered away his future…

Randhir Sobti held back his anger and said. "I'll get back to you." He cut the connection.

The next couple of hours were the longest two hours in the life of Dev Sharma…

✔

Chapter Eleven

(THE AUDITION)

Poonam Chadha looked uncertainly out of the window as the car came to a halt in front of the building.

"This is the hotel?" she asked the driver.

"Yes."

The building was tall and a bit imposing. There was a colorful canopy at the entrance – underneath which stood a muscular and uniformed guard. But the overall impression was not five star.

"This is not a five star hotel?" asked Poonam Chadha.

"No, its three star."

Poonam then looked at her daughter sitting by her side in the rear seat. "What do you say, shall we go in?"

"We might as well, mother, having come so far," replied Pooja Chadha.

The driver turned to face them. "We're blocking the way," he said, his face impassive. "There are three cars waiting behind us on the driveway."

Poonam and Pooja got the hint. The uniformed guard at the entrance of the hotel had been holding the left rear door of the car open for them. The mother stepped out of the car, followed by the daughter.

As the Honda Civic car drove away, the driver pulled out from a pocket his cell phone while steering the car with his other hand. He pressed the speed dial button and spoke quickly to his employer. "They're in the hotel…"

Poonam Chadha walked hesitantly up to the reception desk, followed by her daughter. A short man in a white safari suit (*"They still wear such things in Mumbai?"* wondered Poonam to herself) was standing there, talking to a black suited young man positioned behind the reception desk.

Poonam looked from one to the other, wondering who to address her question to. She did not have to deliberate much on this, since the safari suited man spoke as she approached: "Mrs. Chadha?" Poonam was immediately at ease. She was expected. She was not amongst strangers.

"Yes, that's me. And this is my daughter Pooja."

The safari suited man, who looked like he was in his middle forties, cast an appreciative glance in the direction of the pretty looking Pooja Chadha. "Nice to meet you two ladies! Mr. Shakti Singh is waiting upstairs."

"Upstairs?" Poonam Chadha was surprised.

"Yes. He has hired a suite for the audition."

Poonam swallowed. "Do auditions usually take place in hotels?"

The safari suited man, who had not yet introduced himself, looked stern. "Auditions, madam, take place wherever it is convenient. Mr. Shakti Singh had a script reading session here this morning. He decided to carry on here for his other meetings too." The man's stern look disappeared and he attempted a smile. "The Mumbai traffic is a disaster. It's horrible at this time of the day. Doing all your meeting in one place saves a lot of time and tension."

Poonam Chadha and her daughter had just driven across half the city and had suffered through several traffic jams. She nodded her head vigorously. "I understand – yes, it makes sense to do all your work in one place in a city like Mumbai, rather than keep moving around and get delayed!" She looked at Pooja. "Let's go up, then!"

The safari suited man hastily intervened. "Er – no, madam! Only Miss Pooja will go up. You can wait here – in this very comfortable restaurant here on the ground floor. I will escort Miss Pooja upstairs and then come down again and join you!"

Poonam Chadha again got a feeling that things were going beyond her control a little too quickly. "Why cannot I accompany Pooja?"

This time, there was a slight edge in the voice of the safari suited man. "Because, madam, mothers do not accompany their daughters for their auditions. The aspiring actress must recite lines and act out roles uninhibitedly – which becomes difficult for a first timer in front of the mother. This is our experience – and this is the rule." There was an air of finality in the man's voice.

Poonam Chadha looked worriedly at her daughter. "I'm not too sure…"

Pooja interrupted her mother. "Don't worry, mother. I'm sure it's all right. Mr. Shakti Singh is a very senior actor in Hindi films. I'm sure he knows what's best for me. Let me go up – you enjoy the food in the restaurant. I'll join you once I'm through with the audition."

Poonam Chadha shrugged her shoulders resignedly. This opportunity for Pooja had come after a lot of effort – her daughter had been trying for an acting break in Hindi films for almost a year now. It would be silly to let her middle class inhibitions come in the way of Pooja's big chance, she thought to herself.

"O.K. Go Pooja. And best of luck!"

"Thanks mother."

As Poonam Chadha headed for the ground floor restaurant of the hotel, Pooja and the man in the white safari suit entered a lift in the lobby. They stood side-by-side in uncomfortable silence as the lift rose to the fourth floor. They stepped out into a carpeted corridor. Pooja allowed her escort to lead the way.

The man stopped at a door and knocked. "Come in!" said a strong male voice from inside.

They went in.

The duo stepped into the drawing room of a plush suite. At one end of the room was a luxurious looking sofa set. On one side of the three seater sofa sat a familiar figure – the senior lead actor of Hindi films Shakti Singh. He wore a loose fitting shirt and jeans. On the table in front of him was an open bottle of what looked like Scotch whisky and two glasses. One of the glasses was half full, the other was empty. A plate of peanuts completed the scenery on the table.

Shakti Singh was in a pleasant mood. He saw Pooja look towards the bottle of whisky on the table and said quickly: "I know, I know. It's too early in the day to start imbibing! But you how these script sessions are – so much creative thinking drains the mind and body! A little pep up is always needed after a script session – believe me, it's a professional necessity…"

Pooja had never attended a script session on her life. So she did not know what Shakti Singh was talking about. She adjusted her dupatta self consciously and said: "How do you want me to give my audition, sir?"

Shakti Singh looked quickly at the man in the white safari suit. "You have some other engagement, isn't it, Vinod?"

"I have, sir! Yes, I have. Besides, the mother of this young lady is waiting in the restaurant downstairs. I promised to give her company while she waited."

"Then you must keep your promise!"

The man called Vinod quickly left the room, leaving a tense Pooja Chadha eying the senior actor Shakti Singh with growing trepidation...

Chapter Twelve

(GETTING STONED)

Abhay Kaushik was back in his mansion on Carter Road. He had been discharged from hospital after treatment from shock. He was now recovering from the trauma of almost getting burnt to death in the only way he knew – getting high on drugs in the company of high-class prostitutes.

He had two prostitutes for company this afternoon – Nidhi and Leela. Both were very expensive company: they cost the earth and were high on maintenance, with a taste for expensive clothes and even more expensive perfumes. But they were worth every dime spent on them. They knew how to keep a man happy, all right – happy and ecstatic.

They were also very good company for a drinking and drugs session.

The girl called Nidhi Juneja in particular, not only knew how to enjoy getting stoned – but she also knew all the best and most reliable drug suppliers in town.

One such drug supplier was now sitting with Abhay, Nidhi and Leela at one corner of the massive dining table in the Carter Road mansion. His name was George. He had been carrying a Gucci satchel when he had entered the Carter Road mansion, which he now placed on the table. He had 'professionalism' written all over his face – no small talk, no being in awe in the presence of a superstar, no looking around in appreciation of the lavish surroundings. Just business.

"How many eight-balls do you want?" he asked the prostitute called Nidhi Juneja, who had summoned him with a phone call.

Nidhi looked at Abhay, who made a face. "Just make sure that we don't run out of supply!" Abhay responded.

Nidhi did a quick mental calculation – for her it was a bit of an effort. "Five eight-balls should do it," she finally said.

George stroked his goatee and then opened the Gucci satchel. He rummaged inside and eventually produced five small plastic containers which he then carefully placed on the dining table – in front of Abhay, Nidhi and Leela. "Here are your five eight-balls."

All those sitting around the table understood what the slang 'eight-balls' meant. Each of the five plastic containers contained an eighth of an ounce, or three-and-a-half grams each, of cocaine.

The market value of the contents of the five small containers was about eight lakh rupees.

Leela reached out to pick up a container – but George stopped her with a steely look through his thick framed spectacles. "Money first, please!" The 'please' was added in deference to the presence of the superstar – otherwise George was known to be quite caustic with his vocabulary.

Almost by magic, the star's secretary materialised. He carried a thick wad of bank notes in his hand. "Come with me," he said.

George was assured by the sight of the wad of bank notes in Ravinder Guha's hand. He pushed back his chair, got up, picked up his Gucci satchel and turned to follow Ravinder out of the room. "Have a great party!" was his parting comment.

Abhay just grunted. As Nidhi and Leela reached out for the cocaine, Abhay pulled out a pipe from his shirt pocket and placed it on the table. Nidhi picked it up and opened a container. The fine white powder shined in the glow of the room lights. This was pure cocaine – not street cocaine, which was cut with other substance to increase profits for the drug dealers.

Nidhi filled the pipe with the cocaine powder and lit it up. Abhay took the pipe from Nidhi – and then proceeded to get wasted out of his mind…

Chapter Thirteen

(MAKING PREPARATIONS)

The movie had played itself out on the DVD player. Abhay Kaushik had killed off an entire army of villains in a spectacular climax involving a raging fire in an oil depot and kidnapped school children. The children had been rescued, the chief villain had been burnt alive – the final scene had closed on Abhay and the lead actress of the film Deepika entangled together in a tight embrace and a passionate kiss…

Sanjeev sighed, got up from the sofa and stretched himself all over. In every scene involving Abhay Kaushik he had mentally superimposed the lead actor's face with his own. He, Sanjeev Raina, not Abhay Kaushik, had romanced and sung and fought on the screen. When would the face on screen be *actually* his?

Sanjeev looked at Dev and said: "Enough of sitting around indoors! Let's get out now – Juhu beach awaits us!"

Dev said nothing. His face was expressionless. He just stared at his cell phone.

"How long more are you going to wait for the call?" asked Sanjeev, with some slight irritation. "You can take the call outdoors also…"

"You're right!" responded Dev. He, too, got to his feet. "Let's –" then the cell phone in his hand buzzed.

Dev saw the number flashing on the phone screen and his face lit up. He took the call. "Yes?"

It was Randhir Sobti. "All right," said the head of constructions of Progressive Constructions Limited. "Madam will accompany us. When do we visit your site?"

"I'll call you back in an hour," responded Dev.

The next sixty minutes were some of the most important in Dev's life. He did not move out of the apartment. He made phone call after phone call. An exasperated Sanjeev finally left the apartment to hit the beach alone.

There were many issues to be sorted out before the site visit. Now that the visit was actually happening, Dev needed to put in place the package he had plotted – fast.

"How many small farmers are involved?" he asked during one telephone conversation. "What's the token amount requirement to get the POAs?" he asked later, while speaking to the same person.

Another telephone conversation went like this: "When is high tide? How long does it last?"

During one telephone conversation, Dev had to speak very firmly: "I'm sorry, but I will not proceed with this until I have all the terms signed and sealed on stamp paper! If you lose this opportunity because of unwillingness to complete the paperwork I require, the fault will be yours entirely!"

Eventually, all loose ends were tied up. Then Dev Sharma made one more phone call. "Papa, I need to break my fixed deposit now…" he said hesitantly.

Chapter Fourteen

(THE OFFER)

Pooja Singh adjusted her dupatta again and looked around. The drawing room of the suite was empty but for Shakti Singh and her. "Where are the other people who will take my audition, sir?"

Shakti poured himself some whisky. "They'll be joining us shortly. But I head the panel – I decide. So, as long as I'm happy, you'll clear the audition. A fabulous movie career awaits you, my girl!"

Pooja felt slightly gratified. This sounded positive. She had struggled many months to hear some positive comments like this...

Shakti Singh patted the sofa seat next to him. "Why are you standing like this? Come, sit!"

Pooja crossed over to the sofa set and sat down on a single seater, ignoring Shakti's hand indicating that she join him on the three seater.

Shakti Singh looked slightly irritated at this. His took a large sip from his glass of whisky. "What's your age?" he asked.

"Twenty-two, sir!"

"Ever acted in films before?"

"No, sir!"

"Commercials?"

"A couple – one chocolate ad and one short film on AIDs."

"No raunchy ads? Nothing in a swimsuit?"

Pooja Chadha looked surprised. "No, sir!"

"Why?"

This confused Pooja. "I-I don't understand..."

Shakti smiled benevolently at Pooja. "In films, your body is your temple. The language of cinema is spoken not just with dialogues but also with body language. In fact, the body expresses more than words ever can. If you wish to succeed in films, the last thing you can afford is inhibitions!"

Pooja was silent for a bit. She could not understand where all this was heading. She decided to change the subject – switch to a new track. "Where is the script, sir? Where are the dialogues I need to speak during the audition?"

Shakti Singh put down his glass with an air of finality. "You heard me loud and clear, my dear girl – it's your body language that will take you places more than anything else." He got to his feet. "So let me hear the language of your body!"

A cold hand clutched at Pooja's heart. She jumped to her feet. She now began to realise where all this was headed...

"I-I think I'll skip the audition today, sir!" said Pooja, edging away from the sofa.

Shakti took off his shirt. He was bare chested. "You think I've all the time in the world?" There was a rough edge in Shakti's tone. His voice was slightly harsh, his words slightly slurred. "Come! Let's stop playing games, now! You want to get into films? I'm your only chance to be a movie star! Make me happy – and you'll be made for life!" He made a move towards Pooja.

"Stop!" shouted Pooja. "I'll scream!"

Shakti's eyes blazed. "Scream all you want – this hotel belongs to me! Nobody will disturb us! Now don't make me angry. Co-operate or I'll have to use force!"

Pooja began quaking with fear. This monster was grabbing at her! She reacted instinctively. Her right hand shot up – and she planted a massive slap across the face of Shakti Singh, with a strength she never knew she possessed.

Shakti yelled in pain and went flying backwards. He fell in a heap on the sofa he had just vacated. There was a startled look on his face, as his left hand felt the cheek where the slap had fallen, which was then replaced by a look of great rage. *"You bitch!"* shouted Shakti Singh. "You'll pay for this!"

As Pooja looked on in horror, a knife suddenly appeared in Shakti Singh's hand. He slowly got to his feet.

Pooja should have been paralysed with fear. She almost was. But then an anger began boiling up inside her – a rage at her attempted exploitation. Automatically she pulled out her cell phone from her hand bag – and, in one swift motion, clicked a photo of her tormentor with the phone camera.

Shakti Singh, the ageing and very senior Hindi film actor, was caught on camera bare chested, his eyes blazing with anger and lust and a knife in his hands…

As Shakti shouted and lunged towards her, Pooja turned and ran to the door. With shaking fingers she grabbed the door knob. She swung open the door – just as Shakti reached her. Shakti's momentum prevented him from stopping in time – his head crashed against the edge of the open door. Shakti's eyes rolled up and fell on the floor, blood gushing out from the wound on his head. His head lolled to one side. He was unconscious.

Pooja stood there for a minute, catching her breath. Shakti did not move – he lay prone on the floor.

Carefully, Pooja shut the door on the room and on Shakti. She looked up and down the corridor. There was nobody in sight. Taking a deep breath and holding carefully to her hand bag and cell phone, Pooja walked slowly towards the lift…

Once downstairs, Pooja did not head for the restaurant. Instead, she quickly located the ladies restroom and thankfully took refuge inside. The restroom was empty of any other occupant. That was enough for Pooja – she broke down.

Loud sobs wracked her body for a minute and then she quietened. As she slowly recovered from the shock and horror of her recent experience, Pooja got to work repairing her face with her makeup kit. Eventually she emerged from the rest room.

There was no commotion in the lobby. Shakti Singh was still unconscious – or was he dead? Pooja shivered with the thought and removed it from her mind. The immediate need was to leave the hotel fast!

Pooja located her mother. She was sitting alone at a table, looking a bit worried. Poonam's face lit up as she saw Pooja approach. "Everything all right?" she asked her daughter.

"No mother! Things are not O.K. We have to get out of here fast! Have you paid the bill?"

"Yes, But –"

"Where's the person called Vinod?"

"He's stepped out for some work. But-"

"Good! Let's get out of here!" Pooja grabbed her mother and literally dragged her out of the hotel and into a taxi – all in a space of five minutes.

"What – what is going on?" demanded Poonam Chadha, as the mother and daughter collapsed in the back seat of a taxi and the vehicle moved off.

Pooja ignored her mother and shouted at the taxi driver: "Take us to 'Daily Midday' office in Richmond Avenue in Santa Cruz. *Quickly!*" She took out her cell phone and ensured that the photograph of Shakti Singh had been saved. Then she turned to her shocked mother and said softly: "Shakti attempted to *rape* me, mother. *Now* I'll be a celebrity! *This* is the biggest break of my life!"

Chapter Fifteen

(DISAPPEARANCE)

It was at around eight in the evening that Abhay Kaushik lost consciousness.

The drinks and drugs party which had begun around the dining table in the ground floor dining room later shifted to the mini-theatre located on the second floor of Abhay Kaushik's Carter Road mansion.

In the mini-theatre, a third dimension was added to the party – x-rated films.

The two prostitutes and the film star spent several blissful hours smoking cocaine, drinking whisky and watching blue films. They eventually hit the master bedroom.

Abhay Kaushik was too far gone for further high octane activity. The three settled into a comfortable threesome position on the king size bed and continued imbibing both drugs and whisky.

Abhay was the one overdoing it. He was taking everything in excess – fighting off whatever inner demons that were tormenting him with an overdose of alcohol and dope. The two girls could not keep pace with him – they did not even try.

Nidhi and Leela had their own reasons for keeping their intake of alcohol and dope within limits…

Things were going well. Everybody was, literally, in high spirits. Then, suddenly, Abhay Kaushik, who had been half sitting on the bed and smoking his pipe, gave a low moan – and fell backwards, hitting his head hard on the headboard.

Whether it was the hit on the head or the overdose of drugs and drinks – or both – which caused it, couldn't be said, but Abhay Kaushik had become completely unconscious.

The girls took some time to realise this – they were on their own individual trips. However, it eventually dawned on them that

Abhay was unusually quiet – there was no movement from his side at all.

Nidhi turned to Abhay's prone body and shook him by the shoulder. "Hey! Wake up! What's with you, man?"

Abhay did not respond.

Leela put down, on the nearest side table, the glass of whisky she had been holding and also began shaking Abhay's other shoulder. There was still no response from the actor.

Nidhi and Leela locked eyes with each other. They said nothing – but the message their eyes exchanged was clear. Nidhi quickly picked up her cell phone and dialed Abhay's secretary Ravinder Guha.

Ravinder was in the other side of town, in a bar in a five star hotel, making advances to a young starlet who was eager to use his good offices to get an introduction to his famous boss. When Nidhi's phone call came, Ravinder's hand had already found itself placed firmly on the pretty starlet's thigh. Ravinder quickly removed his hand, however, when he heard what Nidhi had to tell him over the phone. Other priorities immediately took over. The startled starlet was promptly forgotten. There would be other opportunities later...

Ravinder Guha rushed to Carter Road in north Mumbai. It was a relatively long drive. Ravinder Guha's driver did try his best to speed things up without causing a major accident – but the late evening traffic of Mumbai can slow down even the best of drivers.

Ravinder Guha finally reached Abhay Kaushik's Carter Road mansion after 9 pm He found no one. Not Abhay. Not Nidhi. Not Leela.

The three revellers had disappeared...

Chapter Sixteen

(SENSATION)

Pooja Chadha was not as much the sweet innocent that she had projected herself to be in front of Shakti Singh and his sidekick Vinod.

Yes, she had gone for the so-called audition with high expectations. Many months of struggle had given her mother and her a 'clutching at straws' syndrome – they wished desperately to believe every promise of a potential breakthrough in films that was made to them. Of course they had been blind to the intentions of Shakti Singh. They had willfully fooled themselves into believing that the struggle for a break in films was finally going to be over…

But now that the real game plan of the senior actor had been exposed to Pooja so rudely, she had every intention of capitalising on the opportunity that had been so suddenly presented to her by a middle aged power crazed sex obsessed actor's blind and depraved lust.

Which is why Pooja Chadha's first visit, after she fled from Shakti's hotel with her mother, was not to the nearest police station but to the sensationalist newspaper and television channel in which her friend worked as an assistant editor.

Pooja explained her strategy to her mother during the rushed taxi ride to the office of the 'Daily Midday' in Santa Cruz.

Poonam Chadha marveled at how much her daughter had grown up during the last couple of hours…

Poonam's friend from her school days, Sonal Dixit, who worked as assistant editor at 'Daily Midday' was shocked to hear Poonam's story. She also smelt a golden opportunity for her media house. She examined Shakti's bare chested photograph and declared her amazement at Pooja's presence of mind in clicking it under such trying circumstances. The Editor was immediately briefed. Pooja had embarked upon her journey to fame.

The 'Daily Midday' sister concern – the 24 hours news channel on television 'Taza Khabar' – was the first to air the exclusive news scoop. A teary eyed Pooja Chadha was interviewed about her harrowing experience at Shakti Singh's hotel. The senior actor's incriminating photograph – with the knife in hand circled in red – was repeatedly flashed on screen, with penetrating comments on his bare chest and angry face. The other TV channels quickly took up this story, recognising its great potential for generating amongst the public at large great excitement and gossip.

The print media assigned reporters to cover the story of the attempted rape of Pooja Chadha. Preparations were begun to carry the story on the front page – or, at the least, on page 3 – of the national dailies.

Shakti Singh had become the latest whipping boy of the Indian public – not that he didn't deserve it. Worse was to follow. Pooja Chadha, on the advice of the legal experts at 'Daily Midday' and 'Taza Khabar', then paid a visit to the police station under whose jurisdiction fell the hotel owned by Shakti Singh and in which he had attempted to molest the aspiring young actress.

Pooja and her mother were accompanied to the police station by lawyers of 'Daily Midday' and 'Taza Khabar'. The media house also provided, at its own cost, security guards to accompany the mother and daughter everywhere…

The FIR was lodged under full media glare. Pooja Chadha signed her statement with a flourish under the bright lights thrown by the television crewmen. She did not smile at the cameras – she was too smart and too genuinely aggrieved to do that. Her serious demeanor and pretty looks won instant admirers amongst the many thousands of viewers who were watching the unfolding drama on live television.

Pooja Chadha had gone through hell that afternoon. But she had bounced back in style. She had saved her honour with a brave fight and was on her way to ensuring that her molester would face the consequences of his actions as per the laws of the land.

A new star was born that day…

Chapter Seventeen

(THE FORT)

The fort stood majestically on a small island just under one kilometre away from the beach of soft golden sand. Standing at the edge of the small grassy hill overlooking both the stunning beach and the imposing fort in the middle of the sea, Sunita Patel caught her breath sharply.

This was it! This was the dream site she had been looking high and low for all these tiring weeks!

Besides her, Randhir Sobti stood with mouth open and a dazed look on his face. He, too, had been wonderstruck by the site and its immense possibilities...

Sunita turned to the young man who had brought them there. "Who owns this hill we're standing on?" she asked.

"I do," said Dev Sharma simply.

This was not absolutely correct, of course. Dev only held the *power of attorney* on the land. This meant that only *he* could sell the land away – not the actual registered owners. But then, Dev had paid a cash advance to acquire the POA in his name for a limited period of time. If he managed to sell off the land within that period, he would be able to pay off the original farmer owners the balances he owed them. Otherwise, the POA would expire – and Dev would forfeit the advances he had already paid. There would be no refund.

If Dev was tense about the deadline and the connected pressure, his face did not show it. In fact, he looked quite cheerful – a born salesman.

Sunita looked again at the fort. There would be time enough for negotiations later. Right now she wanted to drink in the sight of the fort, the beach, the Ali Baugh coastline and the deep blue waters of the Arabian Sea at high tide.

"Is there a boat service to get to the fort?" asked Randhir Sobti.

"There is *no* service, boat or otherwise!" responded Dev. "We are standing in the wilderness. The nearest trace of civilisation is tiny hamlets of extremely poor marginalised farmers and fishermen who eke out a hand-to-mouth existence."

Randhir Sobti's face fell. Dev saw this and added quickly: "But I've made a provision for a small speed boat. Come with me!"

Sure enough, at the bottom of the hill, after crossing the beach, they found a tiny ramshackle jetty built into the water, which Sunita and Randhir had not been able see from the angle at which they had been standing high up. At the extreme end of the jetty was tied a small motor boat.

The boat was piloted by a man called Rajesh Thorawade. Sunita Patel and Randhir Sobti did not know it – but Rajesh Thorawade was a young and struggling property dealer from Ali Baugh city who had convinced the poor farmers who owned the hill and the land around the beach to group together and sign a power of attorney for their property in favour of Dev Sharma. In return, they had received a cash advance from Dev which was practically half the notional value of the land in this forgotten corner of the world. The farmers had been promised the balance in two month's time – after which they would sign off the sales deeds to either Dev or to whoever he wanted.

Else, Dev would forfeit the advances and the land would revert to the farmers.

It had been a very fair agreement for the farmers – who had no use for the unfertile and partly rocky land and who had never had any hopes or means of attracting buyers to this desolate part of the country. It was Dev Sharma who carried all the risk.

But Dev, as always, knew what he was doing.

Sunita Patel and Randhir Sobti were blown away by the fort.

The approach to the fort had been captivating. The sea was calm, even at high tide. The boat ride was smooth. The sea breeze was cool – and, Dev couldn't help but notice, played elegantly with Sunita's hair, sending strands flying like currents in the ocean. Sunita shut her eyes and lifted her face to the breeze, feeling a sense of calm for probably the first time since her father had fallen so desperately ill...

Dev had to pull his eyes away from the serene look that had enveloped Sunita's quite attractive face. He quickly brought his mind back to the business at hand.

The fort was an experience by itself. It was built of huge stones and covered the entire length and breadth of the island. The fort was surprisingly well preserved, with massive stone carvings of elephants, tigers and peacocks.

Dev saw the look of wonder on Sunita's face and observed: "There are many such neglected historical sites all over India. A few hours of research on the net will reveal names and details of many hundreds of forgotten forts all over the country. This fort is just a typical example."

Dev took Sunita and Randhir to the temple in the inner courtyard and showed them the idols of the various Hindu gods that were carved out of the rocks and still adorned the place after so many years.

"This place is called Kasturi Fort. It is three hundred and thirty years old. It was built by Shivaji and was the seat of one-third of the navy of the Maratha empire." As he spoke, Dev pointed to the hill across the sea, on which they had been standing a little while ago, and said: "If you buy my land for your resort, you will get this wonderful fort and that beautiful beach both free along with the property! You can't get a better bargain for yourself or for your future tourists and guests who will visit your resort. It will be an unbeatable combination for any tourist package!"

Sunita had already realised this. The Daffodils Resorts tie-up would be hers for the asking if she presented the officials of that hospitality multinational the hill and the surrounding land as the proposed site for their first Indian venture. Appropriate investments from both sides would develop proper approach roads and connectivity with Ali Baugh city and then to Mumbai...

This place was a dream tourist destination just waiting to be discovered and developed!

Dev interrupted her thoughts. "We need to get back to the beach. The high tide will recede shortly. Then we won't be able to go back by the boat – until the next high tide."

Sunita frowned. "We'll be stranded?"

Dev Sharma and Rajesh Thorawade both smiled at this reaction. "No," responded Dev. "We won't be stranded. That's the next plus point of this location which I was going to highlight just now. When the tide recedes, there's no water between the fort and the mainland. Your guests will be able to walk from the resort to the fort and back. Better still, you can arrange to keep a fleet of gaily decorated horse drawn carriages – the kind you see on Juhu Beach – to give your guests a joy ride to the fort. They will have a choice of transport – by boat at high tide or horse drawn carriage when the waters recede!"

Sunita Patel and Randhir Sobti gave each other meaningful looks. "Let's get back to the mainland," Sunita told Dev, her hair ruffling in the breeze, her face aglow with excitement. I want to see the waters recede at low tide. Then, we will talk business…"

Chapter Eighteen

(SAVING A FILM)

The mysterious disappearance of the superstar Abhay Kaushik created a national sensation.

The television channels and newspapers were full of reports about the last hours of Abhay Kaushik before he vanished from his home.

The struggling actor Sanjeev Raina was once again very much in the limelight – having saved the superstar from being burnt to death just hours before his strange disappearance.

The news of the over-the-top partying in the mansion during the afternoon and evening prior to the disappearance of the superstar soon leaked out. The servants in Abhay Kaushik's Carter Road mansion made good money from tipping off journalists about the drugs and drinks party. They added their own embellishments to spice up their stories and earn that extra buck.

Abhay Kaushik's persona just kept getting more 'bigger-than-life' than before. Abhay continued to make headline news – in person or in absence.

The police made no progress in cracking the case. There was no trace of the two prostitutes who were partying with Abhay before he vanished. If there had been an abduction – then the three were apparently abducted together.

The police were soon aware of the visit of the drug dealer called George to the mansion – but even this gentleman had vanished. Commissioner of Mumbai Police, Ramesh Tendulkar took personal charge of the case – and coordinated with the Home Ministry in Delhi to sound out a national alert to trace the missing foursome.

The Mumbai police was presented with another sensational headache – the alleged molester of aspiring actress Pooja Chadha and well-known senior actor of Hindi movies Shakti Singh had also vanished.

The lodging of an FIR by Pooja Chadha had resulted in the issuance of an arrest warrant against Shakti Singh. Police were dispatched, amidst full media glare, to Shakti's residence and to his known haunts, including his hotel, to arrest him. Shakti's tearful wife had denied knowledge of his whereabouts. He was not traceable anywhere. The alleged molester had clearly gone underground to evade arrest.

Shakti's sidekick, the man named Vinod who had kept Poonam Chadha company in the restaurant while her daughter was fighting off the lustful actor's advances in the latter's room, had also gone underground. He was also declared a fugitive from the law.

The media went wild. Two high profile vanishings within a few hours of each other was fodder for great attention grabbing news, views and editorial comments.

Pooja Chadha became 'top-of-mind'. It was difficult to avoid seeing her face on television – no matter how avidly one surfed from channel to channel. Pooja was omnipresent, telling her story again and again in channel after channel. Her presence of mind during her torment was praised by all and sundry. The fight and resistance she had put up became a symbol of woman power; her bravery was extolled and her quick thinking that led to the incriminating photograph of her molester was lauded.

In the midst of all this excitement, a producer-director team took advantage of the growing popularity of these two young people, Pooja Chadha and Sanjeev Raina – and quickly hired them for their underproduction film.

Sudershan Joshi and Vijay Bhardawaj had already offered Sanjeev Raina a major role in their film. Now they were suddenly faced with the disappearance of their erratic lead actor. They went into a huddle with their scriptwriters – and came up with a solution. Since a large portion of the film had already been shot and Abhay featured prominently in many scenes, discarding him completely would have meant starting all over again. This would be too expensive. Also, Abhay was now a top news item – his presence in the film would only attract more interest.

So, the scriptwriters did the next best thing – they killed off one lead character and introduced another; a younger brother with a revenge motive. Sanjeev Raina's film career was launched...

Pooja Chadha's case was more complicated. The underproduction film already had a lead actress – and she had not vanished. Divya Parekh was a six-year-veteran of the Hindi film industry with a sizeable fan following.

The twenty-seven-year old Divya was a perfect foil on screen for the thirty-seven-year old Abhay. They had acted together earlier – and had given a hit film. Divya would not take kindly to the introduction of another lead actress into the film. At twenty-seven years of age, Divya Parekh was already beginning to demonstrate the insecurities of a 'maturing' actress. She would tolerate no younger rival in her film...

Pooja Chadha was approached anyway. Sudershan Joshi was too industry savvy to let himself be nipped to the post by a rival film producer. Pooja was news today and a marketable commodity. It made sense to be the first to sign her – she was an aspiring actress anyway and would jump at the break.

Pooja and her mother were delighted. They signed up. The producer was well known. The director, though new, already had quite a reputation and buzz around him. Very big names like Abhay Kaushik and Divya Parekh were associated with the film. Pooja would have been mad not to sign up for the film – as she later explained to her mother, who needed no convincing anyway. Well aware that media fame could be fleeting and temporary, Pooja once again demonstrated her instinctive smartness in grabbing opportunities – and agreed to be a part of the film.

Now Divya Parekh had to be mollified...

Chapter Nineteen

(THE DEAL)

"You're demanding too high a price!" exclaimed Randhir Sobti.

"I don't think so," replied Dev Sharma patiently.

"We've checked. You don't even own the land!"

"Yes I do. I've got power of attorney on all the farm land near the fort – including the hill. I've paid advance to all the farmers. Only I can sell – rather *re-sell* – the land now. The agreements in my favour are all signed and registered in the Ali Baugh District Court."

"We've also found out that you've paid a pittance to the farmers as compared to the price you are now asking from us!" said Randhir Sobti triumphantly.

Dev Sharma continued to be patient. He has known before coming to this meeting in the steel and glass corporate headquarters of Progressive Constructions Limited that he would have to go through these tedious preliminary exchanges of words. It did not matter to him – this was the way all corporates negotiated. He would keep his cool and patience – and wear them out.

"Look, my friend," responded Dev, "it is none of your concern at what price I have purchased the property from the farmers. What matters now is what price I am demanding from you and whether you want to buy at my price. However, you know as much as I do that, before I came along, there was no buyer at all for property in that desolate part of Ali Baugh. Yet I have gone and committed – and paid advance against that commitment – *double* of what the *notional* value of farmland in that area was before I went."

"That's because you saw an opportunity to make a killing from us!" exclaimed Randhir.

"Of course! That's my business acumen! I found out through my research what you were urgently in need of. I discovered this wonderful site – not you. I got the farmers to agree to sell in a group – piecemeal availability of the property would have been of no use for a resort project."

Sunita Patel intervened. "But you're asking us to pay rupees twenty lakhs per acre when you paid the farmers only rupees two lakhs per acre!"

"He did not pay even that!" interjected Randhir. "Our investigations have revealed that he's paid only a lakh rupees per acre to pick up the power of attorney. The balance has to be paid within two months!"

Sunita saw an opportunity. "What if we sit tight for two months? If we wait, and you don't fulfill your commitment as per the legal documents you have signed, the land will revert to the farmers – and we will deal with them then!"

Dev decided that the time had come to cut short what, to his mind, was fruitless conversation. He turned to Sunita. "I will make full payment to the farmers within the deadline," he said firmly, knowing fully well that he possessed not a dime more to pay anybody. The entire amount from the fixed deposit his father had kept aside all these years for his higher education had been paid by him to the farmers as fifty percent advance towards the land purchase. But Sunita did not know this.

"The land will not revert to the farmers," continued Dev. "The land is mine. And if you are not interested to buy from me, then there are many other prospects who would be interested!"

Sunita and Randhir froze simultaneously. They gave quick looks to each other. "What do you mean?" asked Sunita.

"It should be obvious to you! I did my research before I got the farmers near Kasturi Fort to group together and sell to me their individual landholdings as one complete parcel of ten acres. I took a gamble – but a calculated one. In my estimate, my ten acre property is a great site for a tourist resort with a lot of potential. There should be no dearth of interested parties for my property – all I need to do is draw their attention to it, like I did yours. It was I who located the site and showed it to you. You were at your wit's end till then! Likewise, there are many more prospects in the hospitality industry I can approach." Dev paused and then went for the kill. "I can approach the delegation from Daffodils Resorts directly – the same way I approached you. I think they may be interested in my site. If they buy directly from me – you will lose the tie-up opportunity!"

There was a pregnant silence in the meeting room on the fifth floor of the headquarters of Progressive Constructions Limited. Then Sunita tried one last barb: "Daffodils will not deal with you directly. They want a partner in India – a partner of near equal stature. It is the partner who will bring on board to the tie-up the land for the project."

"Maybe and maybe not! I will find out only when I approach them. However, I can also approach the *other* aspiring partners for the tie-up. You're not the only ones!"

This time Sunita knew that she had no bargaining chips left. She realised that she never did possess any bargaining chips to start with. Dev had certainly taken a calculated gamble – he had his fall back options neatly tabulated in his mind...

Sunita badly wanted Dev's property. She had fallen in love with the site. She knew instinctively that the Daffodils delegation would like the site.

Dev hammered the final nail into the coffin. "In case my discussions with you don't move forward, I will next be approaching Buildtech Limited. Ravi Rastogi is keen to snatch the Daffodils tie-up away from you. He's been showing the delegation from Daffodils Resorts some of his sites..."

Randhir was amazed. "How do you know all this?"

"It's my job to know all this, my friend! It's called 'accumulating market intelligence'. How else do you make deals worth crores?"

Sunita gave up. She wanted to prolong the torture no further. She wanted the land Dev had shown her. She wanted the Daffodils Resorts tie-up for Progressive Constructions Limited. And, above all, she certainly did not want Ravi Rastogi, her sworn enemy, the predator waiting at the gates of the company her father had built, to steal the tie-up away from Progressive Constructions...

Chapter Twenty

(THE FRIENDS PROGRESS)

Dev did not budge from his price of rupees twenty lakhs per acre. He took an advance, from Progressive Constructions, of rupees three lakhs per acre – and gave permission for his land to be visited by the Daffodils officials. He realised that if the delegation from Daffodils Resorts did not like the site, it would be unlikely that Sunita Patel would go through with the deal – notwithstanding her personal love for the property he had shown her. In such an eventuality, the advance paid to him would be forfeited by Progressive Constructions – and Dev would still have made a profit of one lakh rupees per acre on his deal with the farmers near Kasturi Fort. And he would get to keep the ten acres parcel of land – for whatever it was worth.

As it turned out, all expectations were met. The American and European officials of Daffodils Resorts liked, very much, the site overlooking Kasturi Fort in Ali Baugh. They had actually lost hope after visiting many less than acceptable sites shown to them by Progressive, Buildtech and some other tie-up hopefuls. The Ali Baugh visit was a complete turnaround. Progressive Constructions had won the tie-up and the joint venture with Daffodils Resorts – provided the Ali Baugh site was part of the deal.

Dev earned two crore rupees on an investment of rupees twenty lakhs. He paid off to the farmers the balance ten lakh rupees that he had owed them. He paid another five lakh rupees to the young Ali Baugh property dealer, Rajesh Thorawade, who had helped in getting the farmers to agree to sell their small parcels of land together to Dev.

Dev Sharma returned to his father the ten lakh rupees he had taken from the fixed deposit his dad had broken to fund his property investment. He sent his father another five lakh rupees as a gift.

Dev was now rich. He now had a bank balance of rupees one crore and seventy lakhs to fund his next ventures...

A few months later, a new looking and shiny Pajero SUV drew up beside police constable Ganesh Chitle, as he was walking down the pavement of Marine Drive promenade, keeping a close eye, as usual, on the crowd of people around him.

The vehicle's front left window slid down. A surprised Ganesh looked into the interior of the red Pajero. A smartly dressed young man wearing designer sunglasses smiled at him from the driver's seat. "Good morning, constable! Remember me?"

Ganesh shook his head. "No. I don't know who you are. And you can't stop here – vehicle parking is not allowed here!"

"Then why don't you get in, constable? I have something important to tell you. Please trust me – this is not a kidnapping!"

Ganesh Chitle took a few seconds to decide – and then shrugged his shoulders and entered the Pajero. Who would want to kidnap him?

As the SUV moved away from the pavement, the young man kept his eyes on the road as he steered the vehicle and said: "Many weeks ago – about six months back, in fact – you woke up two young men sleeping on benches right here on Marine Drive. I am one of them..."

Ganesh Chitle frowned. "I don't think that I remember. I wake up many people sleeping of benches here..."

The young man drew up before Chowpatty Beach, at the north end of Marine Drive, and parked the Pajero next to the pavement, between two other vehicles. He switched off the air conditioning and cut the engine. "No matter. That's not important. I have something more important to discuss. Care for some coconut water?"

Without waiting for an answer, the young man disembarked. Frowning slightly and a bit confused, Ganesh Chitle also got out of the SUV. The young man led the way into the beach.

As they were sipping cool coconut water from green coconut fruit through straws, while standing under the shade of a tree and observing groups of families enjoying themselves at the edge of the water, the young man said: "My name is Dev Sharma. My friend who was with me that morning was Sanjeev Raina. His first film is about to be released – I think next week. It's called 'Aashirwad – the blessing'."

Ganesh Chitle found that a little familiar. He did recollect having seen the promos of a new film called 'Aashirwad – the blessing' on television.

"When you woke us up, that morning, we were just two young men from Dehradun with great dreams but no means. We've come a long way since then…"

Constable Ganesh Chitle finally remembered. "Of course! From Dehradun! Yes, I remember you boys now! So your friend has become a movie star, has he? That was his dream, wasn't it?"

"Yes. He's got what he wanted."

"And you?" Ganesh Chitle looked pointedly at the shiny red Pajero parked at a distance.

"I'm getting to where I want to – making good progress."

"I'm pleased. Good to see young people who arrive in Mumbai with dreams actually achieving success!"

"Thank you! But that's not all that I have to tell you…"

Ganesh lowered his coconut. His face was a question mark.

"For several months now I have been dealing in real estate in Ali Baugh. I have been identifying properties in remote locations of Ali Baugh – preferably near the sea – and have been marketing them to companies and rich people of Mumbai," continued Dev. "A couple of days ago, two of my employees came across something very disturbing. They informed me immediately – and I checked it out last night. There are some funny things happening along the Ali Baugh coast in the middle of the night – the coastline that faces away from Mumbai and out to the open Arabian Sea!"

Gnash Chile's face became very serious. "What kind of funny things?"

"Boats are coming in from the sea, probably from a yacht or ship, and delivering boxes to people waiting on beaches…"

Gnash froze, the coconut water forgotten. "This does not sound good!" He looked at Dev. "Why are you telling me all this? Why don't you report to the police through official channels?"

"Because I *like* you, constable – I regard you as a lucky mascot," replied Dev simply. "After you woke us up that morning, Sanjeev went on to get his film offer that same day and I discovered the property that would help me make my first crore! I decided to give this tip off to you, first, in case it helps further your career. If you wish, then I will go to the police headquarters and tell them right now…"

Gnash Chile raised a hand. "No, don't do that. I will take care of this. Thanks for the tip off! And, by the way, what did you say your name was?"

Chapter Twenty One

(CONSPIRACY)

Constable Ganesh Chitle did not reveal the source of his information. He only insisted, to all concerned, that the source was very reliable. In a police force that relied on undercover sources and informants to crack cases, this kind of information gathering was not uncommon – what was difficult to comprehend was that a low profile beat constable like Ganesh Chitle had developed such an informant…

What Ganesh informed his seniors was very taken seriously – since Mumbai had suffered from several terrorist attacks by the sea route in the recent past. What was not appreciated was Ganesh's insistence that he would reveal the name of the beach in Ali Baugh on which the mysterious landings were taking place only to the Mumbai Police Commissioner in person.

Ganesh made noises wherever he could. Time was running out. If something terrible happened as a result of his informant's tip off being ignored, all hell would break loose…

Eventually, word of all this reached Commissioner of Mumbai Police, Ramesh Tendulkar. Being the man on the hot seat, he could hardly afford to ignore any alarm signal. He met the constable. Ganesh gave him the name of the beach. The location was staked out by undercover police teams. And a great disaster to Mumbai was averted.

The police stakeout paid off. One night, not long after the tip off, there was activity on the beach. Strange men gathered to receive boat loads of boxes. The consignments were taken by the mysterious men by road to a farmhouse in Ali Baugh. The farmhouse was raided.

The boxes were found to contain RDX – one of the most powerful high explosives in the world.

RDX was the main component used in bombs that triggered the serial bomb explosions that rocked Mumbai in 1993, the 2006 Mumbai train blasts and the 2010 Moscow Metro bombings.

Ruthless terrorists had taken many hundreds of innocent lives in Mumbai with bombs made of RDX. They were clearly planning to kill many more...

Many arrests were made in the farmhouse. The information the captives provided pointed fingers to the dreaded Don of Dubai, born in Mumbai and now India's worst enemy – one of the most wanted men in the world, hunted by police of all continents.

Ramesh Tendulkar summoned Ganesh Chitle. "I must congratulate you, constable. You've helped save Mumbai from another terrible terrorist attack! I know I should not ask you this, but can you not tell at least *me* the name of your informant?"

Ganesh had been warned by Dev not to reveal his name. So he had no choice in the matter. "I cannot, sir! My informant is positioned in a very dangerous situation which I cannot explain right now. He gave me the information of the beach landings on the strict understanding that I would not reveal his name. His life will be in danger if it is discovered that he gave the tip off!"

"What are his motivations?"

Ganesh had his answer ready. "He is a true nationalist, sir, but caught in a difficult situation in the underworld as a result of circumstances..."

These words meant nothing, said nothing. The police commissioner was no more the wiser. All he knew was that Ganesh Chitle needed to be rewarded – and that he needed to be encouraged to maintain relations with his very valuable informant.

"Why did you insist on naming the beach only to *me*?"

"Because, sir, as you yourself are aware and as you have announced many times, our police force has more leaks in it than a sinking ship! I did not want any chance of the tip off leaking out and the activities on that beach stopped before we could investigate!"

Ramesh Tendulkar could not negate the wisdom in these words.

Ganesh Chitle was promoted to Inspector, received an increment in his salary and a police medal. This was just the beginning...

Chapter Twenty Two

(TRIANGLE)

At the age of twenty-seven years, Divya Parekh found that her six-year-old film career had been reborn.

When, about six months ago, Divya had been presented with a new lead actor in her underproduction film 'Aashirwad – the blessing' she had been less than impressed. But this lad had turned out to be a phenomenon.

The film had been declared a box office hit and Sanjeev Raina had been lauded as a 'talented charismatic dynamite' by film critics and audiences alike.

The film's debutante director Vijay Bhardawaj also received high accolades – some even comparing him to the genius of yesteryears Guru Dutt, minus the ponytail, of course.

Everybody else connected with the film gained immeasurably in price and stature from the film's popularity, including the two lead actresses Pooja Chadha and Divya Parekh herself.

Pooja's sudden inclusion in the cast had been a major sore point with Divya. Just because that sex crazed crackpot Shakti Singh had wanted to get his dirty old hands on her, Pooja had become a celebrity and a rival, Divya had thought bitterly to herself then. Divya had vowed to fight to the finish – to fight against the inclusion of Pooja in the film.

The veteran of many such casting challenges over many films, the producer Sudershan Joshi prepared a well calculated strategy to overcome Divya's objections to Pooja. He wanted *both* in the film – Divya, because she had already shot many scenes and consumed raw stock and because she had been paid half her fee, and Pooja because of her sudden celebrity status. Also, the film could not be risked on the shoulders of newcomers like Pooja and Sanjeev alone – a veteran with a fan following like Divya was needed to balance out the equation, together with Abhay's somewhat shaky standing, his popularity dented because of his last dud and his erratic behaviour. Abhay's madness and then his sudden disappearance had hyped his charisma – but a genuine star of genuine standing was still needed to balance out the star cast of the film.

So, the script was altered. Divya's role, which had earlier been subservient to Abhay's, was made meatier with the death of Abhay's character. Divya liked the changes and was somewhat mollified. Her character was also made a role model for Pooja's character – which was freshly scripted in and could be moulded and sculpted whichever way was needed.

Pooja would look up to Divya's character throughout the length of the film – and would receive invaluable guidance and advice. This went down very well with Divya Parekh.

What also went down well with the veteran actress was Pooja's behaviour towards her. Pooja was extremely courteous from the first meeting onwards, always respectful, never over familiar, always clearly in awe of the diva that was Divya Parekh. The ego residing in the film star was well massaged – Divya eventually welcomed Pooja into the film with open arms.

Tonight, at the party thrown by Sudershan Joshi in the ball room of the hotel Grand Imperial in central Mumbai, Divya Parekh shared in the glory of the success of 'Aashirwad – the blessing' along with her co-stars and eyed the ever smiling Sanjeev Raina with thoughtful eyes. Here was a newly minted film hero who was clearly marked out for great things – it would do her no harm to link her star to his.

Sanjeev and Divya were standing side-by-side on a small stage, along with the rest of the star cast and the producer and director of the film, posing for photographs being taken by a barrage of cameramen. Divya pinched Sanjeev's left thigh.

As Sanjeev jumped slightly, more at the shock of it than from the sting of the pinch, several photographers caught the pinch for posterity.

Sanjeev turned and stared at Divya, a slightly confused look on his face. Divya gave him a dazzling smile. "How does it feel, Sanjeev – to be the darling of the masses?"

Sanjeev smiled back – but his eyes still carried a question mark. "I'm still getting used to it! A small town boy like me can't absorb too much heady adulation in one go!"

The photographs continued to be clicked, the flashlights lit up the scene of the two chatting animatedly, the TV cameras captured the smiles and the tilt of Divya's body towards her film's hero.

Pooja, too, was on the stage, on Sanjeev's other side. She had been smiling brightly at the cameras – when she noticed a sudden shift of attention. Many of the camera lenses had shifted slightly to her left. She turned her head – and immediately understood the drama that was being enacted. She placed her hand on Sanjeev's shoulder.

Sanjeev jumped slightly again. He turned.

Pooja smiled brightly. "The photographers are really hot for us today, are they not?" she said.

Sanjeev liked Pooja. He still admired the manner in which she had saved herself from Shakti Singh not many months ago. "Yes," he replied. "It's a great feeling – to be the centre of attention like this! A dream come true!"

"Better get used to it! You're a hot and happening film star now, Sanjeev. This attention is going to be a part of your life for a long time to come…" Pooja touched Sanjeev's cheek lightly with her fingers.

The photographers and TV cameramen went wild. Cameras clicked and flash lights went off. TV cameras zoomed in on the two bright new stars lighting up the Bollywood skies.

Divya Parekh's eyes blazed for a split second – and then she regained control. So, thought Divya to herself with sudden realisation, *the bitch had finally shown her true colours!* Divya breathed deeply and made her resolve. *Pooja wanted war – she would get it!*

Chapter Twenty Three

(ANGER AND FRUSTRATION)

Rajiv Rastogi, owner and Managing Director of Buildtech Limited, tore a sheet of paper from the pad in front of him, crumpled it into a tight ball – and squeezed it into the palm of his right hand with all the force he could muster, keeping his eyes closed all the while.

Slowly, the anger and tension that had built up inside him like a volcano on the boil, eased out through the clenched palm and into the crushed ball of paper.

The two men in dark suits and designer ties stood around him in silence. One of the men, Keshav Ratan, his secretary of twenty years, held a glass of cold water in his hand and waited patiently.

Rajiv Rastogi slowly unclenched his hand and dropped the sweat stained and crushed ball of paper on to the floor. He opened his eyes. Keshav Ratan held out the glass of water.

Rajiv Rastogi accepted the glass gratefully and drank the contents in one gulp.

The other two men in the room heaved a collective sigh of relief. The volcano had subsided…

Rajiv Rastogi possessed a gigantic ego – to match with his huge physique. The firing he had just received over the phone had not gone down well with this ego. Yet he could not retaliate – nobody shouted back at a senior lieutenant of the Don. Rajiv Rastogi had listened to the tirade of words from Dubai and had clenched the telephone instrument with murderous rage. But he did not shout back.

The message from Dubai had been clear. The Don was furious at the recent setbacks. His patience was running out…

Rajiv Rastogi had waited for the phone call to be over – and had then vented out his anger on the ball of paper in a time tested method taught to him by a gym instructor many years ago.

Rajiv Rastogi now collected his thoughts and looked hard at Keshav Ratan. "Did you manage to find out how the police came to know about the RDX landings in Ali Baugh? Was it a leak by a gang member?"

"No, boss! There was no leak. In fact, all the gang members are now in jail – *all* of them!"

"They've connected the Don to the RDX landings – that's what the news reports say!"

"Yes, boss! They know that the Don is behind the planned bombing plot. But you're in the clear. Thankfully, the instructions had all come directly from Dubai – the gang had no clue about your involvement and identity!"

"I've been saved this time – but the Don will continue to use me for his missions, in return for the many favours I owe him. I will not be safe until I track down the informant who caused this mission to fail!"

"Only the police will know this, boss!"

"Then alert our informants within the police force. We must find out – the Don insists!"

Chapter Twenty Four

(AMBUSHED)

Pooja Chadha and Sanjeev Raina sat at a corner table in a plush coffee shop located on the third floor of the gigantic Ambience Mall, which is situated on the Delhi-Gurgaon border.

Both were newly minted film stars with easily recognisable faces and a large fan following each. But they were not disturbed by star struck gawkers. The reason was simple: both Pooja and Sanjeev were in disguise.

Pooja and Sanjeev were camping in Delhi with the cast and crew of their second film 'Achiever – the great game'. In Bollywood, nothing succeeds like success. So, the hit pair of 'Aashirwad – the blessing' was once again cast together in the hope that their pairing would continue to set ablaze the box office.

Today's shooting of some action scenes in a location beyond the much hyped Delhi suburb of Gurgaon did not require the presence of either Pooja or Sanjeev. So they had the day off – and the couple had decided to go shopping at Ambience Mall.

Sanjeev needed to purchase tennis shoes and clothes as well as a tennis racket and some tennis balls. He was playing a tennis star in the new film – and needed to do this shopping so that he could look and dress the part. The dress designer of the film would ordinarily have undertaken this assignment, but Sanjeev had volunteered to do so since he had a free day and this errand gave him an excuse to visit a mall with Pooja for some quality time together.

Shopping over and done with, the couple had retired to this coffee shop for some much needed refreshments.

Pooja and Sanjeev really liked each other's company. The chemistry between them was getting better and better with every passing day. Their high comfort level with each other had reflected itself on the screen in their first film together. Their closeness had grown with their success. Pooja and Sanjeev were slowly becoming inseparable.

They were still holding back – each had a burning ambition to reach the pinnacle of success, a desire for glory which made love and relationships and commitments unnecessary distractions.

But the head does not always prevail over the heart.

The two young people shared similar likes and dislikes. They also shared the same profession. They were both good looking and – because of their jobs – were often thrown in close proximity to each other, sometimes in romantic and passionate enactments for the silver screen.

Some of this closeness just had to rub off in real life too. Theirs was a romance waiting to happen…

Today, Pooja and Sanjeev shared the excitement of travelling around in disguise. The make-up artistes in the film crew had done their job well. The couple was virtually unrecognisable. Pooja's jet black hair was now golden brown. Her black pupils were covered by brown contact lenses. Her cheeks were slightly padded. Sanjeev now sported a goatee and thick framed spectacles. The additions and changes seemed minor and innocuous – but they had transformed both Pooja and Sanjeev into completely different people altogether to look at. Nobody recognised them. Nobody amongst the hundreds of people roaming around in Ambience Mall knew who they were.

Or so they thought…

After a relaxed session of coffee and pastries and small talk, Pooja and Sanjeev decided that the time had come for them to return to their hotel in central Delhi and wait there for the rest of the cast and crew of the underproduction film 'Achiever – the great game' to return from the day's shoot in Manesar, a small town beyond Gurgaon.

While Sanjeev paid the bill, Pooja attempted to connect the number of their driver on her cell phone.

Together, they walked out of the coffee shop, shopping bags in their hands, looking like any ordinary couple – not two film stars whose debut movie had just been declared a super hit. Out in the corridor, Pooja frowned. "The driver is not picking up his phone, for some reason," she commented.

They walked towards the escalators in the centre of the third floor lobby. "Where is our driver supposed to be right now?" asked Sanjeev. "He dropped us off at the main entrance. Where did he go after that?" Sanjeev had seen Pooja chatting with the driver while he was getting out of the car – so he had not bothered to involve himself in the details of how they would connect when they planned to leave the mall.

"Our car is parked in one of the basement parking areas – but the driver should be waiting for us on the ground floor, so that he can catch my phone signal on his own cell phone," replied Pooja. "There will be no connectivity in the basement. He knows that. He will bring the car up to the main entrance when I call him – but I can't seem to connect."

"Keep trying – maybe our driver cannot hear his phone because of the piped music blaring through the speakers all over the mall."

Pooja Khanna kept trying, with mounting irritation. She kept dialing the driver's number – but got no response.

"Shall we go down to the basement parking and look for the car?" she finally asked Sanjeev.

"How many levels of parking are there?"

"Good question!" Pooja stopped in front of a security guard and found out. She turned to Sanjeev. "There are three basement level parking areas!"

Sanjeev scratched his head. "Then we'll have to start from the lowest level and work our way upwards. Do you know the car number?"

Pooja shook her head ruefully. "No, I don't know the car number. It's a black Mercedes – there should not be that many around. We should be able to locate the car – eventually!"

Sanjeev smiled sadly. "Let's hope the search doesn't exhaust us!" He looked at the cell phone in Pooja's hand. "Try to connect – one last time!"

It was no use. The driver did not take the call.

Soon, the couple was in the lower third basement. They started walking between the neatly parked rows of cars. Sanjeev held the plastic shopping bag with the tennis racket and tennis balls, shoes and clothes in his right hand. Pooja held on firmly to her hand bag. She had put her phone back in the bag – it would catch no signal deep underground in the basement, anyway.

The lower third basement was unusually empty of people. Not even the parking attendants were in sight. However, the parking bays were full of cars and vans and SUVs.

It was while Pooja and Sanjeev were walking slowly between a row of parked vehicles, trying to spot the black Mercedes, that it happened. There was a loud 'ping' sound as something ricocheted off the bonnet of a Maruti 800 car right next to Pooja.

Sanjeev stared at the hole left behind by the ricocheting object and exclaimed: "Shit!"

He grabbed the arm of a completely shocked Pooja and pulled her to the ground, crouching down himself.

"What – what –?" exclaimed Pooja in disbelief.

"Somebody just fired a bullet at us!" exclaimed Sanjeev, his face ashen. "We have to move from this spot right now! Follow me – and keep your head *down!*"

Pooja simply could not believe what was happening. She simply followed Sanjeev in a bind daze. He was holding her arm so tightly that it hurt. Crouching low, they half ran and half walked between the rows of cars.

There was the sound of another 'ping'. Another bullet had been fired at them! And the bullet had hit one of the cars very near to them!

Pooja's heart jumped to her mouth. She felt sick. What was happening? This could not be for real!

Sanjeev dragged her along, moving faster. She began to slip as she tried to keep pace. Her sari began to unwind. "I can't keep this up!" she cried out, as softly as she could. "I can't keep on running like this!"

Sanjeev stopped. The attacker or attackers seemed to have lost them for the moment. Sanjeev looked up at the Mahindra Bolero MUV whose right side they were crouching next to. It would do...

Sanjeev quickly pulled out a tennis ball from the plastic shopping bag he was holding. Pooja watched in amazement as Sanjeev took out a pocketknife from somewhere inside his jacket, opened it and very quickly made a hole in the tennis ball.

"What – what – are you *doing*?" exclaimed Pooja breathlessly.

Sanjeev smiled tightly and said quickly: "I did a three month commando training course during my last year at college. Let's see if it pays off now!"

Sanjeev reached up and held the tennis ball against the key lock of the door on the driver's side of the Mahindra Bolero, the hole in the ball facing the lock's opening.

In spite of the grave danger they appeared to be in – and her own panicked and breathless state – Pooja was stunned enough to ask: "What's going on? Why have we stopped running? The attackers will catch up with us!"

In response, Sanjeev slammed his fist against the tennis ball, driving all the air out of the ball and into the key lock. Pooja stared in amazement as all the four door locks popped open inside the vehicle.

Sanjeev grabbed the right side door open and pushed Pooja into the Bolero. "Get to the other side, *quick!*" he instructed.

Pooja slid over to the passenger side in an ungainly heap, her sari tearing against the gear lever and her hand bag hitting her head several times in the process.

Sanjeev was about to follow her into the vehicle when Pooja suddenly screamed: "Look out! Behind you!"

Sanjeev swung around. Facing him was an unshaven man with a long nose and a gun in his hand. The gun had a silencer fitted on to it – and it was pointed at Sanjeev!

In one extremely swift movement Sanjeev pulled out the tennis racket from the shopping bag in his hand and smashed it down on the gunman's head with all the strength he could muster.

Blood spurted out from the gunman's head. He crashed to the ground.

In another swift movement, Sanjeev threw down the now broken and useless tennis racket, pulled open the rear door of the Bolero, and threw the unconscious gunman on to the floor between the seats – the blood oozing out of the wound in the head of the thug staining the rubber mats.

Pooja simply stared wide-eyed at the antics of her companion, too startled to speak.

Slamming the rear door shut, Sanjeev jumped into the driver's seat of the Mahindra Bolero and poked his head under the steering column. He found the wires he needed – and the MUV's engine came to life.

Pooja got some of her senses back enough to ask: "Were you a professional car thief at some point before your film career?"

Sanjeev simply grinned, put the vehicle in gear and pulled out from the parking slot.

Another 'ping' sound greeted them – this time the bullet had ricocheted off the bonnet of the Bolero they were sitting in!

There was another gunman around!

Sanjeev raced the vehicle through the lower basement parking hall until he reached a bay leading upwards. He threw the Bolero into the ramp and raced up the two floors until he reached the parking ticket booth.

The barrier was down – blocking the way. The parking ticket attendant looked enquiringly at Sanjeev from inside the booth he was sitting in.

Pooja prayed hard that the wounded gunman on the floor behind her would not now wake up. Why had Sanjeev pushed him into the Bolero in the first place?

Sanjeev pulled down the window and said: "I've lost the parking ticket. What's the penalty?"

Without batting an eyelid, the parking ticket attendant said: "Two hundred rupees, sir!"

Pooja delved into her hand bag and pulled out the hundred rupee notes. Sanjeev paid up, the barrier lifted – and they drove out into the sunshine.

Pooja had never before been so delighted to leave a mall.

"What now?" asked Pooja, as they hit the highway. She looked nervously towards the rear of the vehicle, at the limp form lying on the floor.

"We are driving straight to the DLF City Phase-II police station – it's the nearest one, I think. Anyway, it's the nearest one that I know of! I spent a few weeks in Gurgaon last year, that's how I know. We have to hand over this unconscious gunman to the police – and inform them of the other one in Ambience mall. The thug lying unconscious behind us will, hopefully, reveal who was behind this murder attempt – that's why I took the risk of bringing him along. Please phone somebody from the film crew and inform what happened – and ask some of our people to meet us at the DLF City Phase-II police station."

Sanjeev then looked up from his driving and grinned again. "You may like to adjust your sari before we reach the police station," he said. "Right now it's more off you than on you…"

Pooja's voice was shaking when she replied: "I think I know who the gunman lying behind us is!"

Sanjeev gave her an enquiring look.

Pooja's voice shook further. "That –that's Shakti Singh – the monster who had tried to rape me!"

Chapter Twenty Five

(OVERSEAS ENCOUNTER)

Inspector Ganesh Chitle had been pre-warned by colleagues in the Mumbai police force, who had earlier attended the same short course on investigation theory in Manila that he was now travelling to attend, that Ninoy Aquino International Airport was one of the most chaotic airports in the world.

The first thing Ganesh Chitle did when he got off the plane was to take a deep breath. The next hour would be quite daunting – and so he steeled himself for the struggle ahead.

The first obstacle was the lines into the immigration counters. First timers to Manila, Ganesh had been told by his advisors, attempt to be smart and try to identify shorter or faster lines – and rush to join them. It does not help. You are destined to spend at least thirty minutes in a Manila Airport immigration counter line, no matter which queue you join.

There is no relief when you reach the conveyor belts that bring in the luggage. There are too many bags coming in – you have a long wait ahead, as Ganesh Chitle soon discovered.

The non-Filipino visitor to Manila tends to get amazed at the amount of luggage the overseas Filipino workers return home with. Boxes and boxes of all the latest technology from overseas. These *Balikbayans*, overseas workers, are restricted by rules as to how much they are allowed to bring into the country, although looking at the baggage carousel it is difficult to imagine that any kind of restrictions are applied to them in practice.

Ganesh Chitle had to wait for forty minutes for his three bags to arrive. During that time, he occupied himself with his favourite pastime – observing people.

It was while he was standing next to his conveyor belt, straining to spot his bags among the mass of boxes and other luggage trundling past him, that Ganesh Chitle noticed some Indian faces – in a sea of Filipino and some west European faces.

One of the three men looked familiar – and it irritated Ganesh that his police brain did not register immediate recognition. His mind wrestled with the problem while he simultaneously kept a look out for his bags.

Then it struck him. The face was familiar not because Ganesh knew the man personally. Far from it. The face was known because it featured sometimes in newspaper photographs. And the name behind the face had been sometimes quoted in connection with matters related to the notorious Don of Dubai. This man had even been considered a possible suspect in connection with the RDX landings in Ali Baugh – but no concrete evidence of this had been unearthed.

The man was Rajiv Rastogi, the fabulously wealthy owner of the construction company Buildtech Limited.

He was not alone. He had two bulky and tough looking specimens flanking him. Bodyguards!

Rajiv Rastogi, of course, looked quite capable of protecting himself without the need for any bodyguard. At six feet three inches, he towered over the mass of travellers swarming around him. Filipinos are naturally short – this greatly enhanced Rajiv Rastogi's physical presence in the crowded airport.

Ganesh did not know why he did it – but he turned slightly and tried to avoid being spotted by Rajiv Rastogi. Was it because he, Ganesh Chitle, had been singularly responsible for foiling a dastardly plot of the Don of Dubai – and this man was in all probability a leading lieutenant of that very same international criminal kingpin.

Ganesh did not have to worry about being spotted – Rajiv Rastogi was having a lucky day. His luggage was delivered rather quickly – and he disappeared towards the customs area.

Ganesh, too, eventually got hold of all his luggage. He cleared customs and then headed for the exit, trying to follow the few English language signs.

No one is allowed to enter Manila Airport without special permission, so anyone who is waiting for an arriving passenger will be outside the terminal building, with the masses.

Ganesh's pick-up was waiting – a Filipino driver in uniform with a placard. Ganesh was driven to downtown Manila, to his hotel.

During the entire drive, Ganesh found it difficult to shrug off a sense of unease. He could not put his finger on the reason for this – why was he uneasy?

Could it be that he was uneasy because, for only the second time in his life, Ganesh Chitle had travelled beyond the borders of his own country? Perhaps his sense of unease was rooted in the lack of familiarity with foreign travel – and the fact that the first time around he had travelled with his family and had been only as far as neighbouring Nepal.

This time, he was alone abroad, with no family for support. And he was as far afield as the Philippines – a country with a completely different culture and environment from his own.

Or did the sense of unease stem from the quick glance in his direction that one of the tough looking men accompanying Rajiv Rastogi had given him at the arrival lounge of Manila airport – before the three men had disappeared towards the customs area?

Chapter Twenty Six

(A FUGITIVE NAILED)

The bearded gunman was indeed the fugitive Shakti Singh, who had been on the run from the police for the past one year.

The would-be killer was arrested – and then sent to hospital for treatment.

A hunt was launched for the second gunman and the absconding car driver. They were eventually tracked down – the gunman from a seedy hotel in Delhi's Paharganj area next to the railway station and the driver from his native village in western UP.

The second gunman in the Ambience Mall basement parking had been Shakti Singh's sidekick Vinod, who had also been on the run from the police of the past one year. Once in police custody, he sang like a bird.

The motivation for the attack on Pooja Chadha had been pure hatred, spurred by jealousy at her success and despair at how the lives of Shakti and Vinod had been ruined as a result of her actions.

The duo had been fast running out of hiding places, well wishers and money. Their rapidly deteriorating situation and the news of Pooja's success had ignited a desire for revenge in these two men who had nothing more to lose in life.

The attack had been months in planning. During that time, they had stalked Pooja and kept a track of her movements, all the while evading discovery by the police.

Once the day and place had been decided, the plans had been put in place. The driver had been bought over using scarce resources – but Shakti and Vinod had been driven beyond reason by their hatred and desperate state.

The Commissioner of Gurgaon Police, Rajender Saxena, himself briefed Pooja and Sanjeev in his office, several days after the incident and the capture of Vinod.

"Shakti Singh has recovered from that blow on his head and is now in Gurgaon's Dasna jail, along with Vinod," Rajender Saxena informed the two film stars. "They have two serious criminal cases against them – one in Mumbai for attempted rape and illegal confinement and one here, in Gurgaon, for attempted murder. It is highly unlikely that they will get out of jail for the rest of their lives!"

Pooja shivered. "To think that I had been stalked for all these months by two men with murder intentions on their minds – and I had no clue!"

"You were very lucky, madam," responded the Police Commissioner. "Mr. Sanjeev's presence of mind saved the day. You were attacked by madmen. You have received a second chance in life…"

Sanjeev found it highly amusing that a senior official like the police commissioner, who was old enough to be his father, was referring to him as 'Mr.' but he realised that such things happened with stardom. "We are extremely relieved that Vinod was tracked down so quickly by your police teams," he said to Rajender Saxena. "With both Shakti and Vinod locked up in jail, now Pooja can get on with her life and career without their shadow hovering over her as a constant threat!"

"Rest assured about that," responded Rajender Saxena. "These two will never get a second chance to hurt anybody again…"

Chapter Twenty Seven

(MISCHIEF IN MANILA)

Strategically located at the heart of the Mall of Asia complex in Pasay City, Philippines, the SMX Convention Center is five kilometers away from Manila Airport and, therefore, a popular meeting place for business travellers. As a conference center it is unbeatable – it provides all the technical and infrastructure facilities that may be required by even the most demanding of conference organisers.

The meeting rooms are on the mezzanine floor. It was in meeting room number 11 that the international police training course on investigation theory was conducted.

It was a three-day course, which Ganesh Chitle enjoyed tremendously. He loved learning new things – and his fast track promotion after the RDX landing coup had enabled him to now come into the radar of the training and development department of the Mumbai police force. He was known as a blue-eyed boy of the Mumbai Police Commissioner – and this helped him get shortlisted for plum training courses funded at tax payers' expense.

Now it was late evening of the third and final day of the training programme. The course was ending literally on a celebratory note. Everybody was in high spirits – again quite literally. The bar counter of the restaurant located on the third floor of the Mall of Asia was brimming over with training course participants draped over it. The whole place looked like a mini United Nations. All nationalities and colours seemed to be gathered here – which was almost right, considering the wide variety of backgrounds of the participants that Ganesh had met at the training programme in Manila.

After a while, Ganesh began to feel a little suffocated. He stepped out of the restaurant for a breath of fresh air.

The "fresh" air was, of course, air-conditioned, for he was still within the building that housed the Mall of Asia.

The Mall of Asia, located in the Manila Bay area in Pasay City, Philippines, is one of the largest malls in the world and is as glitzy as they come. Since the training programme classes had been held in a conference center within the same complex so, conveniently, the evening get-togethers were also held in one restaurant or the other located in the Mall of Asia.

This evening's get-together was a special 'farewell' one. There would be speeches galore and handing out of mementoes.

After stepping out of the restaurant that was the venue for the final evening's farewell party, Ganesh went down the corridor for a short stroll.

The left side of the corridor overlooked the ground floor hall, which was vast and teeming with people of all shapes and sizes and ages. Most were Filipino families, but there were people of other nationalities also in the crowd below.

On Ganesh's right, was a row of restaurants and coffee shops and fast food joints. All were glass-fronted, to give passersby a good glimpse of the tempting ambience inside.

It was, of course, rude to stare at people enjoying their meals, but it was difficult not to. That's why these premises were designed as they were, realised Ganesh. Marketing, always marketing...

Ganesh was passing by a glass-fronted coffee shop with half a mind to turn around and return to the restaurant where dinner would be waiting for him, when he saw them sitting at a table and talking earnestly to each other.

Rajiv Rastogi and another man with a dusky complexion and well trimmed moustache whose face looked remarkably familiar.

Ganesh frowned to himself and stopped involuntarily. *Why* was that face so familiar?

And then it struck him like a thunderbolt.

Ganesh's head spun. His mind blanked out for a second with the shock of his discovery. Then he came back to his senses.

Ganesh, like most policemen in India and many Indian citizens also, had seen that face on countless photographs in newspaper and magazine articles over the years. The face Ganesh had just seen was slightly older than the one in the photographs, but it was unmistakable.

Rajiv Rastogi was sitting and talking to the notorious Don of Dubai, the most wanted man of the Indian police forces and intelligence agencies, a man hunted across all continents by Interpol, the man alleged to be responsible for several terrorist acts in the country which had resulted in the deaths of many hundreds of innocent civilians.

Ganesh quickly averted his eyes and hurried on. He did not think they had noticed him. Rajiv Rastogi and the Don were too deep into their conversation, from what Ganesh had been able to make out.

This time Ganesh needed *real* fresh air. He headed to the escalator and the ground floor.

A few minutes later Ganesh was outside.

Ganesh realised that there was no time to be lost. He needed to alert the authorities about the Don's presence in Manila. But *which* authorities?

Ganesh did not know how seriously the Philippines police would take him – the Don was not a wanted man in this country. By the time they had checked the Interpol alerts, it would be too late – the criminal kingpin would have disappeared.

Ganesh realised that his best course of action would be to call the Mumbai police commissioner. He fumbled in his pockets for his cell phone.

Not knowing fully where he was headed, Ganesh kept on walking. The only need he felt was to get away from the crowds – and to make that call to Ramesh Tendulkar quickly.

Ganesh reached the end of the sidewalk. There were lots of people still around him – many carrying shopping bags. He pulled out his cell phone from his pocket and pondered briefly whether to cross the road and then make the call to the police commissioner, away from the noise of the crowd of people around him.

Suddenly, Ganesh felt a push on the small of his back. He was flung forward – and lost his balance. As he fell, Ganesh heard a thunder of heavy wheels. Ganesh turned his head, while still falling, in the direction of the sound.

A huge shape loomed in sight. The truck was headed straight at Ganesh!

Chapter Twenty Seven

And he was falling.

A hand grabbed Ganesh by the waist and flung him backwards. Ganesh waltzed back on to the sidewalk and collapsed in a heap.

The huge truck lumbered past. It had not slowed down a bit. No brakes had been applied. It disappeared from sight as Ganesh lay on the pavement, his lungs gulping in air, sweat dripping from his forehead.

A sympathetic crowd quickly gathered around Ganesh. Someone offered him a bottle of water. Ganesh gratefully gulped down its contents.

Having got his breath back, Ganesh looked up to thank the owner of the hand that had pulled him back from the brink of possible death.

Ganesh Chitle looked into the face of Dev Sharma.

Chapter Twenty Eight

(BUSINESS DEALINGS)

It was just five days ago that Dev Sharma had received a telephone call from Keshav Ratan, the executive assistant and personal secretary of the construction tycoon Rajiv Rastogi.

"We have an offer to make for one of your companies," Keshav had told Dev over the phone.

Dev had been surprised. He had been expanding his business interests by buying up small start-ups with potential, but he had not realised that there would be resale opportunities so early on...

"Which one?"

"'Security Online'".

Dev had a ready answer for that: "Sorry, Mr. Ratan. 'Security Online' is not for sale."

"We will offer you a good price."

Dev was intrigued. "Why do you have such an interest in 'Security Online'?"

There was a pause at the other end of the telephone line. Then, Keshav Ratan said carefully: "Mr. Rajiv Rastogi, who I represent, is keen to expand his portfolio of software companies. 'Security Online' specialises in a niche segment of the software industry. Acquiring it will fill a small gap in the basket of software companies that Mr. Rastogi now owns."

Dev smiled to himself. Yes, his recently acquired company 'Security Online', a small start-up with barely twenty five employees, was, indeed, a highly specialised software company operating in a niche segment with hardly any competitors. That was why he had invested in the company in the first place. The growth prospects of 'Security Online' were mind boggling...

"I plan to nurture 'Security Online' for some years before I sell it off, if at all," replied Dev firmly. "I don't think we can have a deal here."

Keshav Ratan was clearly unhappy. He voice, when he responded, was not friendly. "Think it over. I will call again in a couple of days. Mr. Rastogi normally gets what he wants." The phone connection was cut with an ominous click.

Dev put down the phone slowly, his mind whirring with conjectures. Why was Rajiv Rastogi interested in Dev's software company?

'Security Online' was a firm which engaged in a new software specialisation called 'ethical hacking'. This involved testing the security of a network by trying to crack its systems. The services of 'Security Online' were in great demand – army and navy installations, airports, defence production units, industrial corporations and banks, all had a stake in preventing their online systems and networks from being hacked by mischief makers, competitors and terrorists. They had begun to recognise the great importance of the work of 'Security Online' – its services were becoming much sought after.

Dev froze. Slowly the right buttons were pressed in his mind. Could it be possible that Rajiv Rastogi had reasons other than those purely commercial in wanting to acquire 'Security Online'?

All the rumours and innuendos regarding Rajiv Rastogi's alleged underworld connections, which he had read in newspapers and magazines over the years, began to re-surface slowly in Dev's mind. He felt a chill creep up his spine. Was he overreacting?

Could his company's expertise, in the wrong hands, be used to hack into the security systems of sensitive installations – for dubious gains?

Dev decided that he would take this conversation further, when the call came again after two days, as Keshav Ratan had promised (or was the right word 'threatened'?). Dev decided that he wanted to know exactly how desperate Rajiv Rastogi was to acquire 'Security Online' – and how much he was willing to pay for the company…

Chapter Twenty Nine

(PUTTING THE PUZZLE INTO PERSPECTIVE)

Ganesh Chitle and Dev Sharma rushed into the Mall of Asia and raced up the escalators to the third floor, ignoring the surprised stares of the many people they passed. They were soon standing in front of the glass-fronted coffee shop on the third floor of the mall – the very same coffee shop inside which Ganesh had seen Rajiv Rastogi talking to the Don of Dubai.

The two men – the real estate tycoon from Mumbai and the Don from Dubai – were no longer there.

Dev grabbed Ganesh's arm. "Let's go inside and check the place out very carefully," he said.

It was no use. The coffee shop was half filled with customers. But the two men whom Dev and Ganesh were seeking were not there.

Dev felt Ganesh sag with frustration and delayed shock at his near escape from death. He guided his police inspector friend to a corner table and sat him down. He quickly ordered two cups of coffee from a passing waiter and asked softly: "Are you O.K.?"

Ganesh took a few deep breaths. "I...I think so. I would have felt better if I could have shown you Rajiv Rastogi and the Don sitting here!"

"No matter! You saw them together – that is more than enough! The issue is – why were they together and what were they discussing?" Dev looked carefully at Ganesh and continued: "And why did someone try to kill you?"

Ganesh nearly spilled his coffee. "Somebody tried to kill me?"

"Yes. I think you were *deliberately* pushed in front of that truck..."

Ganesh shivered. "What...what are you *saying*?"

Dev nodded slowly. "I was coming to this mall to meet you. I knew you were here and it was the last day of your training course. I wanted to brief you about a conspiracy I think that Ravi Rastogi is planning – I've been in Manila for two days now investigating this. I saw you about to cross the road and I waved out to you. That's when I saw a tall man behind you reach out towards you!"

Ganesh Chitle remembered the push on the small of his back he had felt just before he was flung forward and had lost his balance. *He had been deliberately pushed on to that road!* He broke into a cold sweat.

"I saw you fall – and I saw that truck racing towards you, almost as if the driver had been waiting for you! I rushed forward to save you!" said Dev.

Ganesh shook his head helplessly. "I know you saved my life – I felt your hand grab me and throw me backwards! But...but why would anybody want to kill me?"

"I only got a brief glimpse of the tall man behind you – before I realised what was happening and rushed forward to save you…" said Dev. "He looked Indian."

"Tall man?" Ganesh again shivered. "The only tall Indian men I can recollect having seen here, in Manila, are the two who were accompanying Rajiv Rastogi at the airport!"

Dev and Ganesh looked at each other speculatively. "Could Rajiv Rastogi have a grudge against you?" asked Dev.

Ganesh's face darkened. "If the Don is connected with the RDX landings in Ali Baugh which I exposed based on your tip off and if Rajiv Rastogi is connected with the Don, which we now know that he very much is, then that could be reason enough to want to kill me as revenge…"

"…on the Don's instructions!" completed Dev Sharma.

The two friends sat for a while in quiet contemplation.

"If Rajiv Rastogi is out to kill you, then you are in grave danger my friend!" said Dev. "You will need constant protection!"

"Yes – I can't depend on you to save my life every time!" Ganesh smiled wanly. "By the way, what are you doing here, in Manila? You didn't come all the way to the Philippines to tip me off about some conspiracy you're referring to!"

"No – that was incidental, because I had found out from Mumbai police headquarters that you were here. I actually came to Manila to check out about Rajiv Rastogi's intentions to buy an online security company in Manila – the only real competitor to a similar company I own in Mumbai, and which Rajiv Rastogi wants to buy from me…"

Dev quickly filled Ganesh in on the background.

Ganesh looked thoughtful. "So, the follow up telephone call from Keshav Ratan regarding buying up of 'Online Security' never came?"

"No – and that got me very worried. I called my competitor here, in Manila – and discovered that Rajiv Rastogi had offered to buy him out also!"

"What the hell is happening?" asked Ganesh amazed.

Chapter Thirty

(A JEALOUS DIVA)

Divya Parekh pressed the remote switch with unnecessary force and shut down the television.

She had seen enough news footage relating to the attempted murder and miraculous escape of Pooja Chadha and Sanjeev Raina to last several lifetimes.

"If Sanjeev hadn't acted as a real life hero, Pooja would be dead by now!" thought Divya Parekh angrily and quite heartlessly.

"If Shakti Singh had not been such a loser and bad shot, she would be free of Pooja and her machinations towards Sanjeev!" Divya continued with her wild thoughts.

Divya threw down the television remote on a nearby sofa and snapped her fingers at a nearby servant for a glass of whisky.

The whisky materialised and Divya used the soothing liquid to calm her frayed nerves.

Divya's obsession with Sanjeev had grown with the weeks and months. Losing out the film 'Achiever – the great game' to Pooja had only added fuel to the already ignited fire. What had started as a flirtatious attempt to win over a budding superstar to further her own career which seemed to have reached a plateau, had eventually grown into a full blown obsession to win over the mind and heart of Sanjeev Raina.

It did not help that Sanjeev showed no inclination to recognise Divya's blatant advances. Rather, he appeared to be succumbing to the spell of that double faced bitch Pooja, who was equally possessive of Sanjeev as was Divya.

Divya sadly recollected how, after the success of 'Aashirwad – the blessing' both Sanjeev and Pooja had signed as many as four films each, two with each other as the lead pair. One of them, 'Achiever –

the great game' was halfway through filming – and the second one starring the pair was about to go to the floors. Pooja and Sanjeev were being forced to spend a lot of time together for professional reasons alone!

Divya, on the other hand, had signed only two films – and none with Sanjeev. She was considered too 'old' to pair up with the new youth icon of the country!

Divya seethed with rage.

Even her godfather, the great Don, was now in no mood to intervene further to push her career. He had done a lot for her when she had been much younger. He now appeared to have acquired newer and younger protégés…

Divya felt like crying. She called out for an another glass of whisky.

As the heat of the whisky warmed her chest and fired up her brain, Divya came to the conclusion that there was only one way to deal with the present problem – and only one person she could approach to make the necessary arrangements for her.

Divya eyed her cell phone lying on a side table. Should she take the irrevocable step?

Divya hesitantly reached out to pick up the phone when it shocked her by ringing. Divya glanced at the number flashing on the screen – and froze. What a coincidence! This was some kind of a divine message!

Her hand shaking slightly, Divya picked up the instrument and answered the call. "Where-where are you?" she asked.

"In Manila," answered Rajiv Rastogi.

"I was about to call you. But you called instead."

"That's good. We still connect somewhere!"

"Don't be sarcastic. I think of you all the time."

"Really? Then why are you never available, these days, when I want some time with you? You have no time to have even dinner with me, much less for anything else!"

"That's not true! My film shooting and dubbing schedules take up a lot of my time…"

There was a loud laugh at the other end of the telephone connection. "Nice one, Divya! That was an entertaining statement.

95

You know you've not much of a film career these days – yet you pretend it's like the old days!"

Divya became furious. Yet she retained her equilibrium with great difficulty. "You seem to forget – my last film was a hit! I've been flooded with offers since then."

"Your last film was a hit because of those two newcomers – and because of Abhay's disappearance mid-way through the shooting schedule and so mid-way through the story. And you're not exactly drowning in new films!"

"Is that why you called me – to insult me?"

"No. I called for something more important!"

Divya decided to ignore this. Her time would come. "I need a favour from you," she told her now-on-and-now-off lover Rajiv Rastogi.

"Good! Then you'll accept my request easily…"

Divya frowned to herself. "What request?"

"I need you to seduce somebody."

Divya once again felt the blood rush to her head. *"I am not your prostitute!"* she shouted over the phone.

Rajiv Rastogi's voice, when it eventually came over the phone connection, was hard. "Yes you are, Divya, you stupid woman! You always have been – that's how you got the Don and me to pave your way into the film Industry. You are not now entitled to a memory lapse! Now shut up and do as you're told! Otherwise, the Don and I can bring you crashing down faster than we raised you!"

Divya calmed down immediately. The combination of bitterness and whisky had made her lose her reason for a while – but she needed to sober down fast now. It would not do to get on the wrong side of the Don of Dubai and Rajiv Rastogi. Besides, she also had a favour to ask…

As if reading her mind, Rajiv Rastogi asked: "And what is this favour you want from me?"

Divya Parekh told him.

Rajiv Rastogi heard her out and then let out a low whistle. "You are a vile bitch, aren't you?" he said.

Chapter Thirty One

(KEEPING TABS)

Mumbai Police Commissioner Ramesh Tendulkar stared at Inspector Ganesh Chitle in amazement. "You've had quite an eventful visit to Manila, haven't you?" he commented.

"It was an unexpectedly exciting trip!" responded Ganesh Chitle.

"According to what you've just told me, you had a very close brush with death! That kind of excitement many of us can do without!"

"Yes, sir. It was an unnerving experience. Also unnerving was seeing the Don of Dubai in the flesh!"

"Sorry to ask this again and again, Ganesh, but *are you sure* you saw none other than the Don of Dubai in person with Rajiv Rastogi!"

Ganesh' face remained impassive. He could hardly afford to show his irritation with the police commissioner. "Yes, sir. I'm sure. The Don's face is familiar to all through newspaper and magazine photographs and television clippings. Also, we know of the alleged involvement of Ravi Rastogi in the Don's affairs – so seeing them together should not be so surprising!"

"You're right, Ganesh. I'm being unnecessarily skeptical. If they – the Don and Ravi Rastogi – are to meet, it will be obviously outside Indian territory. It would be too dangerous for the Don to come to India!"

"Ravi Rastogi, according to my informant, had gone to Manila to try and buy out a company specialising in online security. The meeting with the Don could have been arranged to take advantage of Rajiv Rastogi's travel to a foreign country," surmised Ganesh.

"I have a more interesting thought," observed Ramesh Tendulkar. "Perhaps the meeting in Manila between the Don and Ravi Rastogi took place *in connection* with the purchase of the online security company…"

"This is precisely what my informant also thinks, sir! Ravi Rastogi has also tried to buy 'Security Online', which is a Mumbai based company that specialises in helping organisations build hacker proof online networks. This sudden fondness for online security companies could perhaps have something to do with a nefarious plan of the Don!"

The police commissioner looked at Ganesh speculatively. "Just *who* is your informant?"

"You know that I cannot tell you that, sir! This is a promise I have made to this person."

"But for how long will you keep the identity of your informant a secret?"

"As long as there are spies of the Don or other criminal gangs within the Mumbai police force, sir!" responded Ganesh Chitle a trifle bitterly. "It was obviously an spy from within the police force who informed Ravi Rastogi or the Don or both that I was responsible for the tip off about the secret boat landings in Ali Baugh. That could be the reason behind the murder attempt on me in Manila!"

"You've no doubt that it was a murder attempt?"

"No doubt at all, sir! I was pushed on to the road – and the truck driver was *deliberately* trying to run over me!"

"The truck has not been traced?"

"No, sir. Things happened too fast for anyone to think of noting down the registration number of the truck…"

Ramesh Tendulkar drew a deep breath. "I know there are leaks in the police force, Ganesh. That's why I am having this conversation with you in private. Even my secretary is not going to come into this room until I call for him. The issue is – now that we are clear of Ravi Rastogi's involvement with the Don and we know that something nasty is being planned, how do we monitor activities in that camp without alerting them of our suspicions?"

The two men remained silent for a while. Ganesh than voiced the thought in both men's minds: "We don't know who to trust within the police force, sir! We should look for an infiltrator from outside."

"Easier said than done. Only a professional and highly trained police undercover agent can do this kind of thing!"

Ganesh scratched his chin. "I think I can find such a person from outside the police force, sir…"

Chapter Thirty Two

(THE PROFESSIONALS)

The Goverdhan Thakurdas jewellery showroom in the Karol Bagh area of New Delhi had been preparing for a private showing to the family members of a Marwari millionaire from Jaipur, so there were no customers in the store this morning – just staff members who could open the vault. The thieves chose this perfect time to make their move.

The three thieves wearing fake police uniforms entered the Goverdhan Thakurdas showroom basement through the hole they had drilled in the wall that separated it from the basement next door.

Goverdhan Thakurdas was a world famous jeweller. Its building was secured with a high-tech alarm system and armed guards at the front door. None of that really mattered, though, since the thieves had been drilling a hole every morning for the past one week through the 4-foot wall that separated the jewelry showroom basement from the basement next door.

A woman in the neighbourhood had complained to the police twice in the past one week about early morning noise near her apartment. However, since there was a construction project going on nearby, no follow-up investigation was conducted on her complaints. The police figured that the noise the woman had complained about was coming from the workmen and their activities.

No one took into consideration that the woman lived practically next door to the world famous Goverdhan Thakurdas jewellery showroom.

The three thieves in police uniforms confronted the stunned staff. At gun point they tied up and gagged four staff members. They kept the fifth employee untied so that he could open the safe.

The operation took about half an hour. The thieves netted about five million rupees in diamonds, rubies and gold biscuits.

They tied up the fifth employee also – and returned through the same route they had taken to enter the basement of the jewellery showroom.

The satisfied thieves re-entered the basement next door – and confronted Inspector Ganesh Chitle of the Mumbai police. Ganesh was holding two semi-automatic guns, one in each hand. The guns were pointed at the hole of the tunnel and were the first things that the thieves saw when they exited.

The leader of the thieves immediately recognised Ganesh. How do you forget the man who has once sent you to jail?

Ganesh lost no time in explanations. "If you give me no trouble, I will give you none either. If you listen to me and do as I say, you can keep your loot. But you will have to come quietly with me to a safe house I have nearby, where I can tell you what I want from you. Will you come with me – or shall I alert the Delhi police to come here and pick you up?"

Chapter Thirty Three

(COLLABORATION)

The resort at Ali Baugh had taken a little over one year to build. It looked nothing short of paradise. And that is what it was named – Daffodils Progressive Paradise Resort.

The partnership between Daffodils Resorts and Progressive Constructions was on a roll. Several more super luxury resorts were planned around the country. For location hunting, Sunita Patel turned to Dev Sharma.

Dev readily agreed to collaborate. He had already acquired some very prime properties around the country. He was willing to enter into deals for more…

The grand opening function of the resort was over. The lazy evening sea breeze rustled the leaves of the trees next to the verandah on which Sunita and Dev were standing gazing at the majestic looking Kasturi fort. The Arabian Sea was at high tide – and the fort appeared to emerge straight out of the ocean like some magical castle from a fairy tale book.

"It was good of you to have invited me to this function as one of the guests of honour," Dev told Sunita. "I could not thank you earlier – you were too busy. I'm really grateful that you gave me a chance to participate in this great culmination of your dream!"

"Without you, this dream would perhaps not have seen the light of day, Dev," responded Sunita matter-of-factly. "In fact, you did not know it then, but our purchase of this property from you helped save the fortunes of Progressive Constructions itself. The company may not have survived losing the tie-up with Daffodils. The banks stopped demanding closure of their loans – and some actually gave us fresh loans – when the tie-up got finalised!"

Dev looked at Sunita with a puzzled expression. "Why are you telling me all this?"

Sunita did not reply immediately. She stared at the waves with a strange intensity. She appeared to be on the verge of a decision of some kind. Then she spoke: "You have a business smartness and a business acumen that my father and I need very much on our side, Dev. You've done very well for yourself, even after our land deal. I've been following your career – during the past one-and-a-half years you've converted your profits from our deal into quite an impressive fortune in assets!"

"I've been lucky..."

Sunita laughed. "Modesty does not suit you, Dev. You have a brilliant business mind which you use ruthlessly. You looted us when you sold us this property – but you knew that we would bite your bait because you had done your research well!"

"Why are you praising me so much?"

"Good question!" Sunita paused again, made up her mind – and then made her offer. "My father and I want you to join the Board of Directors of Progressive Constructions, Dev. We will sell you a ten percent share stake from our promoter's stock at a highly discounted price. We want to make you a partner in our journey..."

Dev drew in his breath sharply. He was overwhelmed by the offer. As a director of a blue chip company like Progressive Constructions he would acquire a stature that would otherwise take him perhaps a decade more to achieve. Moreover, a discounted price on ten percent of Progressive Construction stock, which was now on everyone's radar as a share with immense promise of growth, would make him a very rich man from the first day of his directorship.

"What do you want from me in return?"

"That's easy to answer. My father and I want you to put your brilliant mind into taking Progressive Constructions to the next level of success, into helping the company get out of debt – and helping us ward off the takeover attempts of Rajiv Rastogi!"

"You think I can help you do all this?"

"Yes, Dev. I'm certain. Father, as you know, is a very ill. His dependence on the dialysis machine is lifelong. His advice is invaluable – but will not be available forever, I know that..." Sunita's voice choked.

Dev was moved. He wanted to reach out to Sunita and comfort her – but refrained.

The couple stood in silence against the railing of the verandah, admiring the setting sun as it disappeared behind the fort and then into the sea. Then, as a comforting darkness descended, they turned and slowly walked towards the resort building – and towards a future loaded with promise and much more…

Chapter Thirty Four

(OUT OF CONTROL)

Pooja Chadha was driving to her death and she could do nothing – absolutely nothing – to prevent herself from meeting this horrible and untimely end! The car's brakes had failed!

Who would have thought that a simple film shot would have gone so horribly wrong!

The schedule had been arranged in Mahabaleshwar, the picturesque hill resort town about two hundred and fifty kilometers south of Mumbai. The time had come to shoot the climax scenes of the film 'Achiever – the great game'. The entire film crew had shifted bag and baggage to the green hills of this lovely hill station. The film unit had been looking forward to a lot of productive work and some equally memorable fun times. The lead pair – Pooja and Sanjeev – had welcomed this heaven sent opportunity to bond big time. They had become very close after their shared near death experience in Gurgaon – and they had looked forward to their time together in the midst of one of the very few evergreen forests left in the world to, perhaps, take their close friendship to a new level…

Nobody had anticipated this disaster – that, too, on the very first day of the film shooting schedule.

The location was mid-way down the winding road that led from Mahabaleshwar city to the tree lined Venna Lake, which was popular amongst tourists for its boating.

It was nowhere near tourist season, yet, to be on the safe side, a very early morning schedule had been planned, to avoid any crowds and curious onlookers.

Pooja was to be filmed racing away in a car from thugs attempting to kidnap her. The shot was a perfect single take; the director was delighted and signaled for the shot to be canned. But Pooja did not – could not – stop the car.

"What's going on?" asked a puzzled Sanjeev, as he watched the car whiz past him. "Why did Pooja not stop?"

The film's director, Kedar Nagpal, scratched his head. "I've no idea!"

Something clicked in Sanjeev's head. He suddenly rushed forward and jumped on to a motorcycle standing nearby. As he raced off after Pooja, a couple of stuntmen standing nearby sensed the urgency of the moment and jumped on to two other motorcycles that had been readied for the next shoot.

The three men roared down the winding road in a desperate attempt to catch up with the wayward car…

Pooja gripped the steering wheel of the car in terror. It was a Zen Estilo with power steering; so it wasn't difficult to maneuver. *But the car would not stop! The brakes did not work!*

Pooja used her right foot to keep pumping at the brake pedal but to no avail. The brake pedal was useless – the car refused to slow down.

Suddenly, Pooja heard a shout to her right. She turned – and through the open window saw a man in a motorcycle who had suddenly appeared out of nowhere gesturing at her. The man looked slightly familiar but Pooja was in no mood to reflect on where she had seen him earlier. She did not know it then, but he was a stuntman from the film unit who had raced past Sanjeev and had caught up with the out of control car.

Pooja desperately shifted her eyes from the man to the road and back to the man again.

The man shouted.

"What?" shouted back Pooja.

"Why don't you brake?"

Pooja gripped the steering wheel tighter and navigated a turn in the road at sixty kilometers an hour.

"They don't f*****g work!" she screamed.

The man desperately kept abreast of the speeding car while balancing precariously on his motorcycle and screamed back: *"PULL THE HAND BRAKE!"*

Pooja saw sudden enlightenment. She reached out with her left hand and pulled up the hand brake.

The rear tyres of the car immediately locked and the car skidded into a spin. Smoke billowed as the tyres mashed into the asphalt of the road. The motorcycles barely escaped being flung to one side by the wildly rotating car. The screech and scream of tyres scraping the road merged with Pooja's screams as the car slowly but surely came to a stop.

The world went quiet. Even the birds in the trees were shocked into silence. As Sanjeev and the other stuntman rode up in their motorcycles and braked next to the car, the first stuntman, who had already run over to Pooja, pulled open the door and dragged the shocked and terrified film actress out of the vehicle and on to the side of the road.

As Sanjeev raced over to her, Pooja collapsed on the ground and broke into loud sobs...

Chapter Thirty Five

(NO ACCIDENT)

The conclusion was inescapable – the car's brakes had been tampered with.

There were no dearth of car technicians on the sets – the film's climax scenes required several car and motorcycle chases and hence a platoon of highly qualified and experienced mechanics had been kept on standby. The verdict of these experts was unanimous – somebody had deliberately made the Zen Estilo's brakes non functional overnight.

It must have been one of the experts on the film sets. And the deadly mischief must have been done by someone who knew that the Zen Estilo would be put in use the first thing that morning – and, as per the requirement of the script, driven by Pooja. But why would anyone want to cause such serious injury – even death – to Pooja? Everybody was baffled. The police were called in; the day's shooting was cancelled; all crew members were questioned one by one.

There was no breakthrough.

Pooja slept out her trauma– heavily sedated. She surfaced only in the evening.

Sanjeev, in the meantime, turned to his old friend for help. He phoned Dev.

The two friends from Dehradun had come a long way up in life from the time they had arrived, full of enthusiasm but with empty pockets, to Mumbai almost two years ago, to conquer the world. They remained in touch throughout their upward journey which had started unheralded from the benches on Marine Drive. They met once a month for lunch or dinner and found the time to speak to each other on the phone at least once a week. They also shared a project which they had begun around the same time they had got their initial breaks

– and which was nearing maturity. But Sanjeev's phone call now was not related to the project – it was on a more urgent topic.

"Somebody's trying to kill Pooja again!" he told a shocked Dev.

Dev's whistle resonated through the phone connection. "Pooja appears to attract danger like a magnet!" he exclaimed. "First it was the rape attempt. Then the shooting by gunmen in Gurgaon. And now *this*!"

"Shakti Singh was responsible for the first two. But it can't be him, now – or his sidekick Vinod. They're both in jail!"

"Then who?"

"I've no clue, Dev. And I don't have much faith in the Mahabaleshwar police cracking this puzzle. Can you get the Mumbai police on to this case? You have your contacts…"

"I'll try, Sanjeev – for whatever it is worth."

Dev called Inspector Ganesh Chitle and briefed him. "Can you do something?" he asked.

"Of course! Ask Sanjeev to send me the names of all the car technicians amongst the film crew. I'll get a check done on all the backgrounds. I'll also get in touch with the Mahabaleshwar police and get transcripts of the interviews they conducted with each…"

Like all tedious police investigation procedures, the method outlined by Ganesh Chitle sounded extremely unexciting and labour intensive. It was both. But, it was also the most efficient. The computer background checks began in the evening and ran the whole night at Mumbai Police Headquarters. The police commissioner authorised the special activity on the request of his protégé Ganesh Chitle. The background checks threw up a couple of interesting names. A team of experts simultaneously pored over the Mahabaleshwar police interview transcripts with these two suspects. The result was out in the morning.

"Two of the so-called car technicians amongst the film crew are actually gang members of Ravi Pardesi, a thug from Dharavi credited with several murders and kidnappings. He has been in and out of jail, as have these two characters who have infiltrated the film crew in Mahabaleshwar," Ganesh told Dev over the phone early in the morning. "I'll ask the Mahabaleshwar police to take them in for more thorough questioning – but I doubt that they'll know more than the fact that they were carrying out Ravi Pardesi's instructions."

"Then why not arrest this gang leader Ravi Pardesi and question him?"

"A police team has gone to pick him up right now, Dev."

(TRAITOR)

When Ganesh telephoned again an hour later, Dev thought that the call was to update him regarding the arrest of Ravi Pardesi. But the Inspector had called his old friend for an another reason. "Your CEO is fraternising with the enemy," Ganesh told a surprised Dev.

"What do you mean? Which CEO and what enemy?"

"I'm referring to Sudhir Awasthi, the CEO of 'Security Online'. He has been seen visiting the corporate headquarters of Rajiv Rastogi."

"What!"

"Yes, Dev. Rajiv Rastogi's desire for your internet company seems pretty intense. He appears to be buying insider support!"

"Or acquiring technical secrets clandestinely!"

"Yes – you have a traitor in the highest echelons of your company!"

"How did you get to know this?"

"I recruited a three-member gang of thieves to infiltrate Rajiv Rastogi's corporate headquarters to keep tabs on him and try and find out what plots he was hatching with the Don of Dubai and why he wanted to buy up internet security companies…"

"You did *what*?"

"Yes, Dev. I knew the gang leader, Bunty Dubey, from my days as a beat constable on Marine Drive. I once caught him robbing a house on Marine Drive – across the promenade – and sent him to jail. He's become much smarter now – never gets caught. But I caught him – and struck a deal!"

Dev whistled. "You're a real nasty cop, Ganesh! You deserve to go further up the ladder!"

"I know, Dev," replied Ganesh frankly and straightforwardly. "And if I can get to stop Ravi Rastogi and the Don from carrying out whatever tricks they are planning, I *will* go further up the ladder!"

"All the best to you, my friend – but can you complete your story of how you found out that Sudhir Awasthi is passing 'Security Online' secrets to Ravi Rastogi?"

"This guy Bunty Dubey has joined the housekeeping department of Ravi Rastogi's company Buildtech Limited as a superintendent. He has seen Sudhir Awasthi and the film actress Divya Parekh join Rajiv Rastogi for lunch a couple of times in the Chairman's private dining room..."

Dev' mind grappled with this information. "What's Sudhir Awasthi doing with a film actress?"

"One of Bunty's men has been tailing them – it appears that Divya Parekh is very close to Ravi Rastogi and Bunty felt that tailing her could provide vital clues for me. Bunty is really good at this kind of thing – I may actually recruit him into the police force one day!"

"Yes, yes!" said Dev impatiently. "But what is the connection between the actress and the CEO of my company?"

"She's seduced him Dev. He's besotted with her. That's how Ravi Rastogi has got Sudhir Awasthi to betray you..."

Chapter Thirty Seven

(THE ACTRESS AND THE THUG)

Divya Parekh woke up with a jerk to find Ravi Pardesi in her bedroom. She stifled a scream and wrapped the bed sheets around her while quickly struggling into a sitting position.

"What...what are you doing here?" she asked, frightened and angry at the same time.

"The police are on to me. They've arrested my two men in the film unit!"

A cold hand gripped Divya's heart. "You mean they *know*?"

"About you? Not yet!"

Divya regained some degree of control on her senses and studied the thug who had invaded her bedroom. Ravi Pardesi did not carry himself as confidently as she had seen him earlier. The tall and muscular gang leader was unshaven and bleary eyed – and actually looked a little frightened.

"What are you doing here?" asked Divya again, her right hand holding the bed sheets around her and her left hand slowly reaching out to the remote bell button lying on her dressing table.

"I'm leaving the city. The police are after me – they've sent a team to my *adda* in Dharavi to arrest me. I got a tip off just as the police were entering Daharavi – and I managed to escape. I need money. I will go into hiding for a year, probably in Nepal, and I need funds to keep me going while I'm underground!"

"If you're looking for more money from me, forget it!" spat out Divya contemptuously. "I've paid you a small fortune to get rid of Pooja. Rajiv Rastogi told me that you were an expert in this kind of job. I believed him and paid you what you asked for. Now you've bungled it – and put me in trouble! Get out of here!"

Ravi Pardesi's eyes hardened. "If I'm caught, I will tell everything! You won't get away!"

"It'll be your word against mine – that of a thug against a top actress! Nobody can take action against me without proof! Now get out of here!"

Ravi Pardesi made a threatening move forward. Divya's hand reached the remote bell switch. She pressed hard. The buzzer rang outside the room and kept ringing.

Ravi Pardesi stopped in his tracks. He swung around to the open french windows leading to the balcony through which he had entered the room. There was a loud knock on the bedroom door. Divya paused before responding to the knocking on the door. Her eyes locked with those of the thug in her room. She was giving Ravi Pardesi one last chance to make his escape…

There was a glass fronted display window positioned next to the french windows. Several magazines featuring Divya Parekh on their covers were displayed. Ravi Pardesi's right fist smashed the glass and he grabbed a handful of magazines. Then, without a backward glance, he disappeared through the windows and into the balcony…

It took Divya Parekh half a day and a couple of stiff whiskeys to recover from the shock of her rude morning awakening.

Diyva tried several times to call Rajiv Rastogi. But the tycoon did not take her call. The phone kept ringing without an answer. Was Rajiv Rastogi avoiding Diyva?

Finally, Divya decided to take proactive action. She would not be ignored! She had done Rajiv Rastogi's bidding – in return for his help in plotting Pooja Chadha's demise. She had seduced that loser Sudhir Awasthi on Rajiv Rastogi's instruction. Now, that she was in potential trouble for the attempt on the life of Pooja, she would need all possible help from the tycoon who had close contacts with the Don. She would not let him ignore her and cut off communication with her!

A determined Divya got ready and phoned her driver to bring the Mercedes to the front porch of the bungalow. She would drive straight to Rajiv Rastogi's office and confront him!

Divya was shocked to hear her driver's frightened voice. "Madam, something terrible has happened! Can you come to the parking area please?"

Something in the driver's voice alarmed Divya terribly. She dropped the phone and raced to the lobby of the bungalow. Once she was out of the front door, she smelt a strange foul burning smell in the air.

Divya hurried towards parking area. The smell got stronger – and when Divya turned the corner she saw that the foul burning smell had been coming from a car. *Her* car. The Mercedes. Or what was left of it.

All the windows of the car had been smashed, the roof had been ripped off and placed on the rear seats were soggy, charred stacks of what looked like magazines – the same magazines featuring Divya on their covers that had decorated the display window in her bedroom and which Ravi Pardesi had grabbed on his way out.

Divya Parekh realised that day that the burned out shell of a car can be a riveting sight, even if the smoking remains are yours.

Chapter Thirty Eight

(THE PLOT)

You cannot sack, much less arrest, a CEO for getting seduced by a film actress and enjoying lunch with a potential predator of your company.

Dev Sharma wanted Sudhir Awasthi arrested – so he went about gathering evidence of industrial espionage and theft of company secrets against the CEO of 'Security Online' with single-minded focus and dogged determination. For a full twenty-four hour period he did nothing else. The effort paid off.

Dev's technicians discovered that sensitive and confidential files had been copied from the central server of 'Security Online' – files with secret software codes and other classified intellectual property. Very few had access and 'administrator' privileges to these files. The names of those who did have access did not number more than four. One of these 'privileged' persons was the CEO of 'Security Online'. The desktop computer which had logged on and copied the sensitive files was soon identified – it belonged to Sudhir Awasthi.

Sensitive documents and files were missing from the CEO's room and from the high security vault in the IT department. A clandestine search not only revealed this but also, from security records, it was discovered that Sudhir Awasthi had made several night time visits to the corporate headquarters of 'Security Online' in the recent past. Had the sensitive and confidential documents been removed from the premises during such nocturnal visits?

The circumstantial evidence was sufficiently strong, his legal experts advised him, to file a criminal complaint against Sudhir Awasthi with the Mumbai police. Inspector Ganesh Chitle got his opportunity – the CEO of 'Security Online' was promptly arrested and questioned.

Sudhir Awasthi had never expected anything like this. The arrest was a bolt from the blue. The suddenness of it unhinged him completely. He had no clue, till his arrest, that his President was aware of his fraternising with the owner of Buildtech Limited. Sudhir Awasthi had never realised that the missing files and records and software codes would be so easily traced back to him. Confronted with all this evidence, the former top executive of 'Security Online' broke down and confessed.

He had, indeed, been transferring to Rajiv Rastogi extremely valuable and sensitive technical know-how regarding the ways and means of infiltration into internet security systems.

For what purpose?

Sudhir Awasthi did not have a clear idea – except that some kind of cyber attack was being planned by Ravi Rastogi and his henchmen…

Cyber attack?

This is when the information gathered by Bunty Dubey and his two comrades – the professional thieves whom Ganesh Chitle had recruited to infiltrate Buildtech corporate headquarters – proved invaluable.

A large part of the clandestine surveillance conducted by Bunty Dubey and team had involved following Rajiv Rastogi and some of his key henchmen during the frequent visits they kept making to a mysterious bungalow in the Santa Cruz area of Mumbai. Reports filed by Bunty Dubey had described the existence of a couple of extremely high tech rooms inside this bungalow, filled with computers and large machines that looked like complicated electronic devices and network servers used by large organisations to support their internet networks.

It wasn't difficult to put two-and-two together. Clearly, the information stolen by Sudhir Awasthi from 'Security Online' was being put to use in the bungalow in Santa Cruz.

Some kind of a cyber attack was being planned in the Santa Cruz bungalow.

Knowing the connections of Rajiv Rastogi with the Don of Dubai – and the latter's known involvement in many previous attempted and actual terrorist attacks on Indian soil – it was not difficult to deduce that the internet security related activities being fine tuned and planned in the bungalow in Santa Cruz were not friendly or in the national interest. But what was the actual plot?

It was Inspector Ganesh Chitle who pointed out the obvious during a crisis meeting in the office of the Mumbai Police Commissioner. "That bungalow in Santa Cruz is not very far away from Chattrapati Shivaji International Airport , sir!" he told Rajender Saxena and the gathering of senior police officials. "Could this plot have something to do with hacking into airport security systems and networks?"

The room erupted. An attack on the internet security systems of a major international airport had mind boggling ramifications! Hacking into airport – or aircraft – controls could result in major disruption and destruction. The cyber sleuths of the Mumbai police were summoned to contribute to the investigations. The Home Ministry in Delhi was alerted. An immediate raid of the Santa Cruz bungalow was planned...

A fleet of ten police jeeps raided the mysterious bungalow in Santa Cruz. There were a couple of guards at the entrance – who put up no resistance to the massive police team. The occupants of the bungalow were caught completely by surprise by this swift action. A total of twelve people were rounded up. Two of the arrested men, although well disguised, were quickly unmasked by the police experts in terrorist identification. They were leading members of the Srinagar based terrorist organisation *Lashkar-e-Tayyeba,* the largest and most militant Islamic jihadi movement in south Asia, banned by many countries including the US, UK and India and the outfit behind the 2005 Delhi market bombings, the 2006 Mumbai train blasts and the 2008 south Mumbai attacks.

Alarm bells rang across the length and breadth of the Indian security establishment and top government circles. Over the next twenty-four hours, the country's best cyber brains converged on the Santa Cruz bungalow. It did not take them long to crack the plot.

The plan hatched by the Don of Dubai and the *Lashkar-e-Tayyeba,* with the active connivance of their stooge Ravi Rastogi and his organisation, was to take control of the aeroplanes taking off from and landing at Mumbai's international airport and force them to crash with newly invented computer software.

The key to the plot was acquiring expertise in hacking into the security network of Mumbai's Chattrapati Shivaji International Airport, located in Sahar, which was very near to the Santa Cruz bungalow that had been taken over by the terrorists. The next step was to take over the controls of select aeroplanes by remote control.

When Rajiv Rastogi's attempts to buy out the two top companies in the world specialising in cyber security, one in Mumbai and one in Manila, failed due to Dev Sharma's intervention, he hit upon the idea of stealing the expertise. Sudhir Awasthi was co-opted for this, using the seductive charms of Divya Parekh – and the information supplied by him had gone a long way in taking the terrorist plans almost to the verge of fruition…

The timely action by the Mumbai police and Inspector Ganesh Chitle, aided and abetted by Bunty Dubey and his two thieving colleagues and Dev Sharma, had prevented the world from witnessing the horror of many passenger aeroplanes, their controls compromised by remote control through computer software, dumping all their fuel in mid-air or taking a nose-dive immediately after take-off or just before landing. The lives of thousands of innocent passengers and crew had been saved…

Chapter Thirty Nine

(A CHAPTER CLOSES)

The police laid siege to the steel and glass tower in central Mumbai that housed the corporate headquarters of Buildtech Limited.

The Chairman of the company, Rajiv Rastogi, was holed up inside the building. The police had come there in force to arrest him on charges of waging war against the state – a crime punishable with death.

From his thirteenth floor office, Rajiv Rastogi could see the forces of his doom gather in the driveway and compound of the headquarters of his company.

There were Indian paramilitary forces also gathered outside the building, together with the police contingents. The armed soldiers and policemen surrounded the corporate headquarters of Buildtech Limited in a tight embrace. Nobody was allowed to leave or enter the building. The uniformed soldiers and policemen outside the steel and glass building were armed to the teeth.

Ravi Rastogi turned away from the ground-to-ceiling window and looked around his lavishly appointed suite of offices for one last time, knowing well that the end was near.

His phone was no longer ringing. He was untouchable – nobody, not even his most trusted employees, those who were still not in police custody – would venture to talk to him and put themselves in further danger.

The Don of Dubai had cut off all contact.

The great real estate tycoon was on his own now.

Rajiv Rastogi's life flashed past him – a medley of business coups and terrorist activities. And, of course, the killings – on behalf of the Don of Dubai and the *Lashkar-e-Tayyeba*. But then, if not for such patrons, how could he of such humble origins have risen to such great heights? Could there have been another way?

It had all come crashing down now – the castles he had built on the foundations of blood that he had spilled. The only issue that mattered now was – how would it end? In the deep darkness of prison and in the horror of the gallows?

Rajiv Rastogi already knew the answer. He had already loaded the pistol. The gun was gleaming on the top of his magnificent desk – mocking him.

His hand shook as he reached out for the instrument of his demise.

The sound of the gunshot rang out loud and clear – splitting the air with a note of finality.

Chapter Forty

(THE ANGRY MOTHER)

There was a good reason for Poonam Chadha to make a pact with the devil – the very man whose henchman had tampered with the car's brakes on the film sets in Mahabaleshwar in an attempt to kill her daughter Pooja.

She intended to prevent further murderous attempts on her daughter's life.

Poonam Chadha did not smile as she handed over the briefcase to Ravi Pardesi. "There's one lakh rupees inside this briefcase," she said, her eyes cold. "The balance two lakh rupees you will receive when the job is done. Then you can disappear to wherever you want!"

Ravi Pardesi also did not smile as he took charge of the briefcase. "The job will be done. You will have your revenge!"

"You'd better make sure that I *do* get my revenge! Don't mess it up!"

Ravi Pardesi did not respond. He had his own reasons to do the job that he was being paid so generously for. The payment was a bonus – which would help fund his disappearance and subsequent stay in Nepal for one year.

Poonam Chadha had been shocked when Ravi Pardesi had made his sudden appearance in the penthouse apartment Pooja had purchased with the recent earnings from her blossoming film career. She had been even more shocked to hear his story. "You tried to kill my daughter – and now you're asking for money to escape!" exclaimed Poonam Chadha. "Are you mad?"

Ravi Pardesi told her what he would do in return. Poonam Chadha was further shocked – and then intrigued by the possibilities. Ravi Pardesi's confession had planted a deep hatred towards Divya Parekh in the heart of Poonam Chadha. That jealous bitch had tried to kill her daughter! She would have to pay!

Poonam's late husband and Pooja's father had retired from the Indian army as a full colonel. He used to always maintain that those who lived by the sword normally died by the sword. Now, Poonam Chadha could not agree more...

It was three days later that the employees of Bharat Roadlines Transportation Company in Ajmer noticed a foul smell emerging from a large parcel that had been delivered to their warehouse from Mumbai the evening before. The parcel was found to contain an iron box. Inside the box was found the highly decomposed body of a woman...

Sensation.

The autopsy revealed that the woman had been drugged before being brutally stabbed several times. Her face had been destroyed by acid. She could not be immediately identified.

The Mumbai police investigated the office of the transport company where the parcel had been booked. The name and address recorded in the register of the man who had delivered the parcel, for transportation to Ajmer, were found to be fictitious. The address in Ajmer to which the parcel had been booked was also found to be fictitious. The police had reached a dead end.

Nobody then connected the dead woman found in Ajmer to the mysterious disappearance of the film star Divya Parekh. This connection was established, to the shock of the entire nation, once the DNA test results were out and the police investigators did some intense deducing. By then, Ravi Pardesi had long disappeared into Nepal...

Chapter Forty One

(SECOND CHANCE)

Dev Sharma stood on the edge of the parapet overlooking the Doon valley. About 30 kilometers in the distance, deep in the middle of the lush green valley was his home town Dehradun. Dev could not, of course, see the town from this distance high up in the Mussoorie hills, which was just as well. The orphanage, rather village for parentless children as his father called it, in the lawns of which he was standing, was as further away from the hustle-and-bustle of everyday city life as a mountain spring is from a busy river port.

All around Dev was the sound of joyful laughter – the glee of children in a playground. On the slopes were scattered small cottages, fourteen of them, in which these children lived. None of these children had known their parents – they had all come to this place as babies and small infants, referred by government agencies and social workers. They were growing up as brothers and sisters, ten to a cottage, under the loving care of a 'mother' – a professional care worker who had dedicated her life to this mission. It was in this 'children's village' that a hundred and forty helpless penniless orphans had received a second chance in life.

A simple and beautiful concept – funded by the former superstar of Indian cinema, Abhay Kaushik, who had gone missing in Mumbai three years ago.

Sunita Patel, who partnered Dev in all his business ventures these days, had also come with him on this trip to his hometown and to the 'children's village' his father had created on the hills of Mussoorie. Right now, Sunita was sitting in a chair in a nearby lawn, chatting animatedly with a group of 'mothers' who sat on chairs or on the ground around her.

Dev heard somebody call out his name. He turned to see Ravinder Guha, the secretary of the former superstar Abhay Kaushik headed his way with the distinguished looking gentleman who was his – Dev's – father.

Dev's father carried the personality of a charismatic elder statesman. He was distinguished looking, with a thick head of white hair – and displayed a permanent twinkle in his eyes. Dev envied his father his steady state of happiness – and was also grateful for it.

Dev had not known his mother, who had died during child birth. His father had never re-married, preferring not to burden his baby son with a step mother. He had brought up Dev singlehandedly, while also nurturing young minds as a professor in Dehradun's only college. He had retired five years ago after serving the same college as its principal for a decade.

The 'children's village' was a dream project Dev's father had carried in his heart for about twenty years or so. He put all his retirement benefits and life savings into buying a small piece of hillside in Mussoorie and built the first three cottages. He soon ran out of money but managed to struggle on with donations from former students who had made good.

Dev had gone to Mumbai to make his fortune so that he could help support his father's dream. It was as simple as that.

The only other major investment Dev's father had ever made was a fixed deposit to fund his son's higher education.

It was this fixed deposit that Dev had used to fund his first real estate deal – the Ali Baugh farmland which he had leveraged into a small fortune.

What had also helped stabilise the 'children's village' project and enabled it to grow into a fourteen cottage complex was the donation Ravinder Guha had arranged from the estate of his boss, the film star Abhay Kaushik…

Now, both Dev's father and Ravinder Guha carried broad smiles on their faces. Dev's heart lifted. "He's agreed?" asked Dev.

"Yes," replied Ravinder Guha, grinning from ear to ear. "Your father convinced him. Abhay is ready to return to Mumbai and to films…"

Chapter Forty Two

(SALVATION)

It was Ravinder Guha, the long suffering secretary of Abhay Kaushik, who had taken decisive action, three years ago, to save his boss from the path of complete self-destruction he had set himself on.

What had helped Ravinder Guha in embarking on this enterprising act of becoming his employer's saviour was the fact that Abhay Kaushik, in one of his saner moments, had given his trusted and loyal secretary power-of-attorney over his financial affairs.

So, Ravinder Guha could afford to spend lavishly to save his boss.

Having come to his decision, Ravinder Guha had contacted the young man who had recently saved his boss from burning to death. He had gambled on Sanjeev's innate decency to prompt him to help out. Ravinder Guha was not wrong in his estimation. Together they hatched a plot to remove the berserk film star from Mumbai.

Sanjeev Raina could think of no better place than Dehradun, his hometown. He asked Dev for help.

It was Dev who had immediately seen the possibilities – for Abhay Kaushik and for his father. He had unashamedly asked Ravinder Guha for a large donation for his father's 'children's village' and he had asked his father to use his considerable influence to place Abhay Kaushik in an ashram in the Himalayan Mountains, not too far from Mussoorie.

The rest of the arrangements were done by Ravinder Guha. He set up an elaborate plan to drug and then transport Abhay Kaushik half way across the country in an ambulance to the ashram near Mussoorie. The drug dealer George was adequately compensated – he now owned and ran a hotel in Kathmandu, away from the clutches of the Indian police and with plentiful supplies of drugs to cater to his addictions. The two women who were partying with Abhay Kaushik before he disappeared were also now settled in Kathmandu – partners in a flourishing beauty parlour that Ravinder Guha had financed.

Abhay Kaushik had woken up in an ashram high up in the mountains overlooking Mussoorie. The ashram's presiding spiritual guru was a doctor who had given up a thriving private practice in his mid forties to search for God and enlightenment. Now, at the age of eighty, he was a formidable spiritual force with many thousands of devotees in India and around the world.

Abhay Kaushik was quickly captivated. His salvation had begun…

Chapter Forty Three

(DREAMS ARE LIKE STARS)

It was six o'clock in the morning. Dawn was slowly crawling red-eyed over the horizon, touching the calm grey waters of the Arabian Sea with little streaks of yellow light. The sky also lightened slowly, giving promise of a new day with new hope.

Three men stood quietly on the pavement of Mumbai's Marine Drive promenade, in companionable silence, staring out at the ocean waters, drinking in the opening act of the new day and ignoring the stares of passing joggers and morning walkers.

The stares were more for Sanjeev Raina – the new superstar and number one actor of Indian cinema – than for anybody else. Sanjeev's latest blockbuster, in which he had co-starred with former superstar Abhay Kaushik, who had made an amazing reappearance cured of his self-destructive streak and arrogance, after being missing for almost four years, had broken all box office records. Abhay Kaushik had earned a second lease of life in Bollywood while Sanjeev Raina's was now the most well-known face in India – it would have been strange if the morning visitors to Marine Drive had not recognised him. The blockbuster was also Dev's first foray into film production.

"This is where it all began, four years ago," remarked Sanjeev softly, closely watched by his bodyguards who stood a little distance away, but near enough to be able to rush to protect their boss in case of any apparent danger to his person.

"The journey's far from over, my friend," responded Dev Sharma, also under close watch by his gunmen standing at a respectable distance.

Police Superintendant Ganesh Chitle, promoted immediately after the busting of the terrorist plot to crash passenger aircraft at Mumbai's international airport a year ago and whose police bodyguards were also positioned alertly in the vicinity, gave a short laugh. "You own quite a bit of Mumbai already, Dev. And now that you're engaged to Sunita, you stand to own quite a bit more together with her. You've also become a successful film producer. What further journey do *you* want to make?"

Sanjeev laughed and looked fondly at his childhood friend from Dehradun. "If I remember right, Dev, that morning we first met Ganesh at this spot four years ago, you said something about owning this whole city, no less!"

Dev smiled and decided to change the subject. He eyed a group of young girls in jogging gear headed in their direction like heat seeking missiles. "Your attempt at early morning anonymity is not working, Sanjeev. You have fans headed in your direction. I think it's time we headed out of here…"

The three men turned to move towards their respective cars parked on the side of the pavement, drivers in position behind the steering wheels, engines idling and ready to rev up at short notice. Sanjeev could not resist a last comment.

"You're closely following your father's advice, aren't you, Dev? He used to say that dreams are like stars…"

"…you may never touch them, but if you follow them they will lead you to your destiny," completed Dev. "Perhaps I *am* following this philosophy, Sanjeev and Ganesh, but so are the both of you…"

The young girls reached Sanjeev and surrounded him. His bodyguards kept a watchful eye as the film star signed autographs on pieces of paper thrust at him with practiced ease. Ganesh and Dev entered their cars and drove off, soon followed by Sanjeev, each towards their eventual destiny…

THE END